The Voice In the Gowi

Some of the book's
main characters

The Voice In the Govi

Gérard A. Besson

Paria Publishing Company Limited
"Tall Stories"
Second Avenue, Cascade
Trinidad and Tobago
pariapublishing@gmail.com
www.pariapublishing.com

Typeset in Dido Regular
Printed by Lightning Source, USA.

ISBN: 978-976-8054-87-6 (softcover)
ISBN: 978-976-8054-88-3 (hardcover)

Contents

1. La Sirène Rosa:-

OU PÒKÒ TWAVÈSÉ LAIVYÈ; PA JIWÉ MAMAN KAYMAN.
You have not yet crossed the river—do not curse the crocodile's mother.

They had sent for her, it was after midnight. She knew
they would. It was not that they did not know what to
do, but they wanted her. She stood for a moment in
the quiet street, its darkness hardly punctuated by the
dim yellow glow of the now burning low street lamps. A
warm wind carried an odour of cesspits and poverty.

In the distance a cock crowed mightily. He was answered by a ragged cacophony of his freshly awakened
comrades, their early morning voices trailing piteously.

Inside were two women, she could see them through
the window that opened on to the street; they seemed
to move like moths about the blackened pitch oil lamp
that burned on an old-fashioned sideboard.

"Is he do that," hissed the old woman as La Sirène
Rosa entered the room. "Is heself, Antoine Paseau, ah
want you to fix him." She spoke the Patois of Grenada
and smelled of red lavender. "She didn't want him again,
he too damn bad. Then he send this for her." It was a
pretty pin cushion, red, of the sort that the Tobagonian
peddlers sold. "The day she get it, she take een."

1

The priest had come and gone. The incense, burned during the rite of Extreme Unction, lingered in the little bedroom in which Marie-Aurélie now lay dead in a single bed. Her sister Eliza and her old mother Eloïde had already brought in the tub, half of a wooden barrel. In the water, limes cut in half, black sage and leaves of Jumbie balsam floated.

Working together, the three washed her quickly, turning her frail pale yellow body over, and over again. They washed her face; her dead eyes, open, regarded their averted looks. They parted her thick black hair to one side, combed and brushed it, laying it prettily on her bony shoulders.

They had handled her well. Nothing had drained from her.

"You going to close her?"

La Sirène Rosa had already taken several neatly wrapped parcels from her handbag.

"Eloïde, here, I want you to do this part."

"No, not me," said the old woman. "Not me." She rubbed her hands against her thighs, as if drying them. "Not me Rosa—she is my child, oh God! But I don't want to close her . . ."

"Come, Eliza, help me with this before rigor mortis sets in." Three soft candles were swiftly stripped of their wicks.

"Look the mortar," said the old woman. Rosa shredded several leaves off of a bundle of black, damp, pungent tobacco. She put these, together with a bunch of garden balsam and six or eight lumps of charcoal, into a small apothecary's mortar, and ground the mixture with a heavy marble pestle. To this she added the soft candle. Scooping out the mixture, she kneaded it in her hands and placed a quantity of it into the dead girl's vagina and anus, then into her ears and nose.

"Put the cloth on your sister, Liza." Eliza, with shaking hands, passed the folded white cotton cloth between the dead girls legs. "Here, tie her feet, and pass this one under her chin and tie it on top her head."

"Look, this dress, use this dress, she liked this dress." The old woman was now weeping silently, tears streaming down her lined and tired face.

"Ah Bondyé, Bondyé."

"To close her eyes, Eloïde," murmured La Sirène Rosa.

"Here." She handed the old woman two copper pennies, new, they bore the profile of Queen Victoria as a mature woman.

"She must not look back."

"Close her eyes, Eloïde," said La Sirène Rosa, "close her eyes good." With trembling fingers the old woman pressed the dead girl's eyes closed, and placed the shining copper pennies on them. The lamp light flickered, giving the impression that she was wearing spectacles. "Rosa, Rosa," the old woman whispered, "I want you to mount this, I want you . . ."

"Not now Eloïde, not now, everything in time."

The old woman, her hands shaking, held two long wooden whips, stripped of their barks, one from a calabash tree, the other known as mayama bush. "Take it, Rosa, take it, take them."

"Send the boy with them later. Liza, I want you to take the sweet soap and this hairbrush of hers and use them, they were your sister's, and take her dresses. Take the one she wore to church last week."

"Rosa, the little boy . . . ?"

"Yes, Eloïde, bathe him in this, her water, but in the morning, warm it up. Bathe him and say one Our Father and five Hail Mary's. Tomorrow, let his grandfather pass him over the coffin three times, one for the Father, one for the Son, and one for Holy Ghost. Dig a hole in the yard and throw the remainder of her water in it, don't bother to bring it to Lapéyrouse to throw in the grave. Little Pierre-André will be alright, as for Antoine Paseau, his father, send the whips. Liza, sweep, eh, sweep everything in that corner by the bureau, in the morning collect it, and send it for me. Just wrap it in some Gazette paper, and send the pin cushion too."

"The man from Haynes Clarke reach, Mammy." It was Eliza's daughter. "They bring the box."

"Let them come," said the old woman. The rites for her dead daughter now ended, her sense of control was returning. Outside could be heard the sounds of the hearse, and horses stamping, their trappings making metallic noises. A tinker suddenly called "Sharpening knives and scissors!" The bedroom door opened, polite strangers, differential, un-met eyes. Eloïde felt relieved.

Later that morning, before family and friends, neighbours and those who follow wakes in an almost professional style arrived, La Sirène Rosa returned with the whips, they were now stained red.

The cathedral clock struck noon, the household knelt about the small room to say the Angelus. Marie-Aurélie was laid out in a plain pitch-pine coffin, freshly varnished, which was placed in the middle of the drawing-room upon two dining room chairs that faced each other from the opposite ends of her coffin. Her little face was wreathed in jasmine. She, in her pretty white Irish linen frock with its crochet trimming, laced with a pink velvet ribbon, looked excruciatingly young. Eliza put her sister's first communion cards and her confirmation certificate into the coffin. They were her credentials and passport. She wound around them a white ribbon to which was pinned the medals blessed by the parish priest, Father Latour, given to her when she received those sacraments.

"You are a good girl, Marie, a good good girl, God will see that, you have all your papers, God will see that, you hear, Marie-Aurélie. Don't mind them, don't mind them."

"Put these in her hands," said Rosa, passing the red stained wooden whips to Eloïde. "Now put a clean handkerchief over them, no one needs to know your business."

"Thank you Rosa, Thank you. God bless you. How will we ever repay you . . . ?"

"No, no, hush, you have nothing for me." Rosa held her close and patted her back as she would a child.

La Sirène Rosa didn't stay for the wake. Already the house of mourning was filling up, people in black, purple, gray and mauve were fanning themselves, the late afternoon heat raising their mingled perfumes in a commotion of vapours, heady and charged with dreadful memories of commonly held tragedies and bereavements past, present and anticipated.

◆ ◆ ◆

The first lash hit in his heart, it felt like he was being pierced by an ice-pick. Antoine Paseau was just leaving his grandmother's house on Duncan Street to go to Naza. The blow staggered him, he felt surprised and confused and forgot himself and sat down on the wooden steps just outside the bedroom door. The pain ebbed. He had sweated through his shirt and the old black jacket. He saw his hat on the ground, it seemed far away. He felt he had not the strength to reach for it. He felt cold and there was a tingling sensation in his face and the back of his head. He hugged his knees as a sense of fear began to replace the confusion. The next lash took him across his back. A sharp burning pain that drove him to his feet, he turned to run back into the house just as the bedroom door slammed shut. In a frantic effort he grabbed the edge and tried to pull, that was when the first stone crashed into the side of the house. He bawled, but there was no sound. Turning, he saw the large white stone on the step, next to his foot, it had come from the stone bleach, a pile of boulders in the form of a square that was used by the household to whiten clothes upon in the blinding light of day. Another rock, bigger, just rose from the pile and struck him on the shin. He bawled and tried to scream and run. Something struck him hard across the face, spinning him about. He stumbled, fell, rose to flee as three, four, large white stones struck him hard on the arm and chest and leg.

The bleach was stoning him. The other one caught him on the jaw. He tasted blood and gasping spat out teeth. Several more stones struck him forcefully on the head, body, and face. He fell, and still the rain of stones continued, covering him, piling up about him and the wooden steps until the entire stone bleach had transferred itself to bury him beneath it, all heaped up very neatly on the side of his grandmother's house. Then stillness. Several tiny white butterflies danced in pairs in the bright noon light above where the stone bleach once had been.

◆ ◆ ◆

La Sirène Rosa walked slowly, enveloped in a sense of weariness, from the little house in upper Prince Street towards Brunswick Square, and sat for an hour or so on a bench before the newly installed fountain, admiring the way that the lingering sunlight caught and illuminated the spray in a prism of colour surrounding the beautiful nude female form that topped the fountain.

She could hear the drums for bongo. The lamp lighter had tipped his hat to her, the old, wrought iron lamps around the fountain cast hardly a shadow. "That's not my funeral," she thought. They would dance for an hour or so, and then Captain Baker would send a constable to issue a warning for disturbing the peace.

She grew up in a hat, as they say. This meant she did not tie her head as black women did. She had 'good hair.' She did tie her head though, on occasion. To pray. For fasting. Or, to lock herself away, sometimes alone. At times with another person. She tied her head to dance the bélè with my grandmother, who also tied her head, although she did not need to. La Sirène Rosa's style of dress was in those days à la Capresse; a costume that my grandmother wore only on occasion. "Come," she said to the empty space beside her, "it's time to go home."

She stood amongst the small crowd of the farcical and the curious and looked as a coffin passed. It was balanced on the head of a huge black man, a Nèg Guinée, a black from Africa, with fixed and staring eyes in a face that appeared as though carved from very hard wood in another country. They were taking Antoine Paseau, that same night, to the hanged man cemetery. No church for him. People said it was a case of suicide. The body packed in quicklime lay inside the box, eyes open. He was looking back. In the shadowy crowd of hats and umbrellas, it was drizzling that evening, she could see Naza. She knew him as a Bokor, a practitioner of black magic, an Obeah-man. He was a small ugly person, effeminate, with a grinning face.

The people said he was a Congo and that he had been brought to Trinidad as a child, taken from a slave ship, and set free. None of which was the case. They said that he had grown up in Saint-Anne, in St. Elizabeth Village, with the remnant of the former slaves from the Coblentz estate. This was closer to the truth. They called him Naza because he had 'powers.' He was perceived by them as the inheritor of an antique and long enduring evil that harked back in time to slavery days, perhaps before. This in fact was so.

Antoine Paseau, the one in the box, had been his thing, his creature. Rosa felt convinced, however, that it was he, Naza, who had dispatched Paseau to seduce Marie-Aurélie, and that it was Naza himself who put upon her what the people call 'a wanga,' a magical charm of the most wicked intent, which caused a terrible and debilitating illness to afflict her when she would not follow Paseau any longer, or keep company with him in the abandoned estate house at the top of Gonzales Hill. Of these things she felt sure. The poison, and it was a poison of some sort, was not in that little red pin cushion. Marie-Aurélie died to show everybody that 'the Naza' was a man of power, not to be contradicted or trifled with.

◆ ◆ ◆

That night, La Sirène Rosa, who lived in a wooden three-bedroom house at the back of my grandmother's house on Belmont Circular Road, which was opposite to the Carmelite Convent, brought into the sitting room a large tin bath pan. She closed the front door, locked it, and closed the two front windows, making sure that the jealousies were shut tight. She filled the bath pan with water heated on a kerosene range in the outhouse. With slow and careful movements she removed all her clothes and stepped into the warm water, into which was strewn a quantity of basil leaves that she had crushed; their scent filled the room. She rubbed her face and neck, arms, breasts and body with the crushed leaves, next her legs and her narrow feet. She then soaped herself all over with a new cake of Pears soap.

She felt the need to purify herself, to be made clean.

The two lamps that she had lit burned clear and bright, one in the middle of the small, round, elegant dining table, the other on a matching sideboard obviously made in the previous century. The room was austere. No pictures on the walls, no curtains. There were three straight-backed bent-wood chairs with cane seats and a sofa to match. Two very old arm-chairs, their gold-leaf peeling, stood on either side of the sideboard. A white circular crochet doilie decorated the table, illumed by the golden lamp light, and another long one the sideboard. The lamps themselves, heavy, cut-glass bowls, made by Val Saint Lambert of Belgian, were enhanced by tall, slender chimneys. The walls were painted white, and the pitch-pine floor scrubbed well over many years.

She rose from her bath as the water cooled. Her hair piled upon her head, bits of basil leaves sticking to her long, slim brown body. She was finely made. Now forty-two, "a massissi," a word used in Saint-Domingue to describe a woman who is a lover of women, she had had many "les amies," friends.

There was once a man in her life, though. A good companion. A protector, a sometimes lover, with whom she lived, on occasion, in "plaçage." Her own béké, an aristocrat, a wealthy one. Twenty-seven years her senior, this Frenchman had once been a business colleague and friend of her father's, Louis Rémy.

She had been little more than a child when Claude-Ambrose du Vivier de Noailles became a frequent visitor to her mother's home. With great discretion he befriended her like a kind uncle, and brought her Martiniquan dolls and sugar cakes. He sat in a straight-backed chair stuffed with human hair, sipping anisette liqueur from a tiny crystal glass, listening to her sing French madrigals, as Mademoiselle de Paralon played the piano in the upstairs front room of their home on the Calle de San José, or, as the French inhabitants of Port-d'Espagne knew it, la Rue de la Place, later called George Street.

The house was next door to what would become the Angostura Bitters factory, but was then the Presbytery of the Roman Catholic Cathedral of the Immaculate Conception. Claude-Ambrose read fairy stories to her, and the fables of Jean de La Fontaine, in French, as they sat together in the old drawing room on breathless afternoons. He taught her the courtly dances perfected by Raoul Auger Feuillet, the tambourin, the passepied and the gavotte, how to eat nicely like a lady and how to curtsey before royalty, and the social nuances which distinguish those to whom she should offer her hand to be kissed.

Her mother, Ursule Bridgette, had been herself a child of the New World custom of the plaçage, generally referred to as 'les mariages de la main gauche,' or marriages of the left hand, in which European men of substance and women of colour entered into long-term arrangements that would over time produce a beautiful race, les gens de couleur, . . . "à coup sûr, les meilleures et les plus douces personnes qu'il y ait au monde." Thus, Ursule Bridgette encouraged their friendship and gave comfort to their innocent liaison, in anticipation of the enchanting honey-coloured golden child that would one day be the product of their love.

When she became sixteen years of age their relationship matured. She would let down her thick, jet-black hair about her naked shoulders, and he would know her virgin thighs. She never took another man and he only ever knew his wife and La Sirène Rosa. Her womb would not quicken for him, her one regret. For having only sons he would have loved a daughter. A lovely sang-mêlé, a belle-bois, a girl who would grow like a pretty tree, a doux-doux for his old age who would have lent perfection to their plaçage.

She and my grandmother would be friends and lovers for over fifty years.

That night she took care to perform her toilette with an elaborate formality in her bedroom, with two tall candles burning on either side of her dressing table mirror. She sat erect as she brushed her hair with a silver-backed hairbrush that was made from lion's mane. Never losing sight of her eyes, she braided it up, with arms, round, held high, while glancing to admire the charming uplift of her breasts. She felt the slight draft that made the candle flames waver, lighting her shoulders in shifting shades of dusky rose and sapodilla.

She tied a dark maroon ribbon close around her neck, and as a consequence transformed herself in such a manner that made her smile in admiration. Her crisp nightgown smelled of vètivè as she stepped onto her high old bed, the candles burning steadily, lighting the eyes of the subject of a tall painting, rendered in oils and framed in gold-leaf, of a beautiful European woman dressed in the costume of the ancien régime, and settled herself into the freshly laundered white linen, exactly in its middle, around which four huge mahogany carved posts stood like sentinels.

Her thoughts turned to a certain old object in her keeping. It was her true inheritance actually, and was symbolic of past existences. Called 'the Govi', it was her most cherished possession. The Govi, a simply made clay pot, was kept in a larger, more ostentatious receptacle and contained, in a symbolic manner, the accumulated history of her own life—her mother's, her grandmother's, even her great-grandmother's, as well as intimations of her people's experiences through times long past.

Her meditation led her into those places never travelled with conscious clarity, places that were the reservoirs from which she drew the energy, the wisdom that directed her waking life. This other place, this self, submerged deep within her inner being, ever hardly remembered, was in truth her eternal twin, her soul, or, as the Patois-speaking people of these islands would say, it was her 'Gros Bon Ange'. Her great good angel.

This 'Gros Bon Ange' was the well and the spring of her abilities, it was the source of her intelligence, intuition, and wit. A precious gift that had been preserved over generations. It was her mother's gift to her, which she, in turn, had received from hers as her own true inheritance. This gift conveyed the capacity to conceive beyond actuality, to desire beyond capability, to create beyond need. It was the result of labour, a careful cultivation to ensure that nothing from life's experience, conscious or unconscious, became lost, that even after death, the reclaiming of the soul of the one who had gone to the waters beneath the Earth, may be retrieved from the invisible spirits, the souls of the departed who dwell there. This work was called 'Retirer d'en bas de l'eau.'

1. LA SIRÈNE ROSA

This was, by no means, the sentimental worship of long dead ancestors, nor did it have to do with the past per se. It was a method by which her people retrieved and incorporated the best of past lessons and experiences into the present moment, and as such kept the past as progress made. A foundation was formed, from which one could deal with the future. In La Sirène Rosa's world, the living did not so much pray for the dead, as have the dead help sustain the living.

The Govi held not just the 'Zemi,' the spirits, of her mother Ursule Bridgette and of her grandmother Erzulie Freda, but also their fetishes, personal objects and lucky charms. It was a reliquary for Erzulie Freda's mother, her great-grandmother, a woman of the Rada people of West Africa who had seen her daughter taken and carried away into slavery. The Govi, La Sirène Rosa knew, was the place that honours woman as the divinity of life's vision, Erzulie Freda, Goddess of Love, the muse of creativity, after whom her grandmother was named. The Govi contained objects from Africa and others that originated on the island of Saint-Domingue before the winds of revolution had driven Peletan de Molé and his child Ursule Bridgette to this distant island, named for the Blessed Trinity.

The defining moment of La Sirène Rosa's life was when old Tanti Cyrillia, a childhood friend of her mother's, had placed into her hands a gorgeously-made jar, decorated with a depiction of the Blessed Virgin Mary accompanied by the Archangels. This jar contained the Govi that held the relics and the fetishes, the symbols that so potently evoked the accumulated memories of her ancestral past. This had been some years after her mother's death, and had followed the ceremony that reclaimed her mother's Gros Bon Ange from the waters under the Earth, the dwelling place of les morts. This inheritance, this source of strength and life, these ancestresses in the Govi, over time, were transmuted from being merely a collection of personal objects into a crucible for La Sirène Rosa's beliefs: they symbolised the accumulated memory of her people, their 'Gros Bon Ange'. These evolved from the respected mementoes of loved ones to the revered artefacts of individuals who became luminaries, possessed of oracular voices that spoke from the Govi directly to the heart of La Sirène Rosa Rémy.

◆　◆　◆

"Marie-Aurélie is not dead, listen, Eloïde, do not say a word, just listen."

Outside, the Crier Mally was just beginning her wailing, nasal chant to announce the deaths of the day. "Marie-Aurélie Clément is dead. She was the oldest child of Miss Eloïde, the short chabine Grenadian woman who use to sell mamee seepote in the market. She fadder was Papits the white Bajan overseer who use to work for Mr. Carry. Her sister is Eliza, the dark girl who is wash for Madame Maupertuis. The funeral is from the house of mourning, four Prince Street and then to the Cathedral and straight to Lapéyrouse cemetery. Amen.

Bless your ears and inform the necessary." Already her voice was trailing away, only to begin again near to Fauré Street by the entrance of the Eastern School at the back of the market, where an open savannah that was called Savane Céduine stretched all the way to the edge of the Dry River.

"Your child is not dead."

But Eloïde, her mind already teetering on the brink of senility, was now to step into the dark with-drawing room of lunacy, and hover there in the bric-à-brac of her confused past.

Eliza understood full well. She knew that her sister, long ago, had fallen under the spell of Antoine Paseau; slipping away in the heat of the day to do what?

"To take her soul? Liza, her Gros Bon Ange that is part of the soul, the part that you have, I have, the rest belongs to Almighty God."

"Why—? How could they do that, Rosa?"

"Well, they start with her, with she, her self; the 'Ti Bon Ange,' her personality, that was weak, you know how she was—why? Work of the devil. Antoine give her to Naza. Now Naza want Marie-Aurélie, he want her body. He will dig her up from her grave tomorrow night and make her a living dead, what they call in Saint-Domingue a zombi, he will use her and then sell her down the Main. We mustn't let him get her, Liza we have to hide her— too much people in the house. Go, tell them time to go, and close the door, don't let in more people, no more praying for today. Tell them your mother fall down, she weak, she don't want anybody till the funeral. Go quick, Liza, I have to see about your mother."

Eloïde stood there like a statue, hearing but not knowing, a wild hysteria growing. Rosa came prepared.

"Eloïde." La Sirène Rosa spoke in a voice of command. "Drink this." The small blue bottle contained a powerful opiate. "Open your mouth!"

The old woman, her eyes staring in different directions, wouldn't.

"Come, Eloïde, I don't have time, open!"

The struggle was soon over. She would sleep for the day.

"They gone?"

"No, Iodène still here and her daughter."

"Call Iodène."

"Iodène, Miss Rosa calling you."

"Iodène, send home your daughter, I want you to help me here, do not ask me anything today. Just do what I tell you. And keep your mouth shut."

Iodène, who had crossed herself at least fifteen times already, whispered, "She gone, Miss Rosa, ah tell she to go and iron clothes for the funeral."

Marie-Aurélie's limp, ice-cold body was taken out of the coffin where she had lain from the day before. "Oh God, Miss Rosa, she so soft. She ent get stiff. She ent dead. Oh God, oh God, Miss Rosa, the priest, let we sen for Father Latour."

1. LA SIRÈNE ROSA

They laid the girl out on the narrow bed. Rosa, removing the substances with which she had closed her orifices the previous day, covered her with two blankets after placing a sealed ware jar filled with hot water at her feet.

Eliza, covered in cold sweat, could not utter one word.

"We will send for Father Latour later. He must know what is taking place, and will have his work to do. — Change her dress. Come Liza, Iodène help her. Do not let anybody in here. All you stay, I'm coming back just now."

La Sirène Rosa returned to the house of mourning with a very large quantity of a bushy shrub called locally grain amba feuille, seed under leaf, a plant with thousands of tiny seeds. This she stuffed into Marie-Aurélie's empty coffin, and fastened the lid shut. Rosa worked assiduously as there was still much to do.

♦ ♦ ♦

You see, it was that night, following the "death" of Marie-Aurélie, when La Sirène Rosa had meditated upon her ancestral relic, the Govi, that she had been disturbed by the sound of stones being knocked together in a quick staccato. It was a summons, she understood that. Standing at her window she could see the first of them running up De Castro Lane, at the back of her house.

Les Cochons Sans Poils; the pigs without fur. Naza's people. 'Bête Sereine,' the animals of the night, his society of sorcery dedicated to mischief and the work of the devil. The people said that they could turn into pigs or rats, a big donkey, even an enormous snake. "They does eat people." They were now running down Rudin Lane, heading for the Dry River, the shortcut to Sainte-Anne; flambeaux burning in the wind. Three, with cow-horns strapped to their heads, dressed in dry banana leaves; the one in front, short, thick, sort of hopping backwards, that was Naza. She drew back from the window. She knew he knew that she was watching him watching her.

She slipped outside, crossed the dark backyard and passed through the little wicker gate that divided her yard from my grandmother's.

"Amélie," she called to my grandmother softly beneath her open window. "Open for me."

They sat together in our drawing room, my grandmother in the rocking chair next to the blue majolica vase, La Sirène Rosa on the piano stool, quite close to her.

"Sleep, Amé, sleep for me, please, dream and tell me, we must now know about Marie-Aurélie's death."

When the dream came, Amélie entered, wondering, into the comfort of her most still self. Her most receptive self. The self that listened to the soul of the world. Soul to soul, until the vision of Rosa's family's relic from slavery days, the Govi, filled her whole dream. Its rim a wheel, the wheel a well, the well a mouth, the mouth a womb, the womb a grave, the grave, the grave of the world. To Amélie's soul came a voice, the voice was her own, and theirs, all of Rosa's mothers, one speaking like a child, in a child's voice, others a little quicker in the Patois of Saint-Domingue, and another in a strange language. "This," said the voice of an old person, "is where it had all begun."

Amélie sighed deeply and began to speak:

"In a place of coincidence, at a time of fate, your grandmother, Erzulie Freda, and Zinga, the father of Naza, commenced a journey, traveling on the same wheel. Marie-Aurélie has suffered a false death brought about not by magic but by a chemical substance, a secret substance found in the glands of a fish that blows up like a bladder. The poison paralyzes all muscles and stops the person who has eaten it from breathing. Some live longer, for a day, if they live the day, they come back. Some people stay unconscious for days.

"The magic of the Bokor, Naza, is a trick, a powder made from the glands of the fish. It was administered to Marie-Aurélie. She inhaled it as a powder, as Antoine Paseau made love to her in Naza's hideout in Gonzales Place. She had eaten it. She had good days, and bad turned to worse, and dramatically from one day to the next she was at death's door."

Amélie sighed heavily, moaned, and started to rise, but fell back on the rocker.

"Look, see Dr. Comparriol has come, there is nothing he could do," she shook her head violently, "she fading.

21

They calling the priest, the light gone from her eyes, her face fall. Eloïde bawling, tying up her belly and sending Eliza for Rosa Rémy. You come, you on the same wheel as Naza, Rosa Rémy.

"Now tell her!" said Amélie in the other another woman's voice, speaking with difficulty in the Patois of Saint-Domingue. "Make it plain to her the wickedness and evil that is being done. Tell her the secret the Spanish priest used."

Amélie opened her eyes, she was fully awake.

"Rosa, it is Naza, he is creating a zombi out of Marie-Aurélie. First she had to 'die' and then he would take her from her grave and sell her as a slave to the ones who traffic in the un-dead. It has come to me; I will tell you what you must do, once and for all."

◆　◆　◆

In the half-light of the shuttered bedroom La Sirène Rosa sat by the still form. With her inner eye she regarded all that lay there. The body, not yet corps cadavre, but alive, skirting the outer frontier of death. Comatose in the power of the drug, which by its evil nature allowed the sufferer to hear all, understand all, and be terrified by the rites and ceremonies, indignities and painful regrets that they would believe was the experience of what it is like to be dead. They would think that their spirit has lingered in the gloaming of this world, to listen to the grieving of the ones they love and to anticipate, as a punishment, the terror of what is to come.

La Sirène Rosa took a small face mirror from her bag and held it to Marie-Aurélie's nose and mouth. At first there was nothing, but after several minutes the faintest mist appeared, and as quickly vanished. There would not be another for a long time. Rosa, bending forward into the shallow light, passed her little finger across the mirror, there, it left no trace. She listened, with an ivory stethoscope, one flattened end to the girls chest, the other to her ear, there was no sound. There was no pulse. Yet the 'zétwal' of Marie-Aurélie, her highest spiritual self, the one that dwelt, not in her, but above, her destiny, the map of her past travels, the chart to journeys sailed, the star that guides to the final quest, still lingered.

The Gros Bon Ange, her angel, linked to the Almighty God, had by the power of the drug, and by Marie-Aurélie's belief in the magic of Naza, been made weak. Her Ti Bon Ange, her self, her character, her individuality, had been overcome and taken over, there was no will. She believed that she was dead. The 'Nam,' the spirit of the flesh that allows each of her cells to function, her body to work, had been banished, leaving only the form. These elements of life's endeavour must now be harmonised.

La Sirène Rosa opened her little prayer book and prayed silently 'Deliver me, O Lord, from my necessities; see my abjection and my labour, and forgive me all my sins. To Thee, O Lord, have I lifted up my soul: In

Thee, O my God, I put my trust; let me not be ashamed. Glory be to the Father, to the Son and to the Holy Ghost, Amen.' She prayed so as to give herself strength to deal with Marie-Aurélie as the drug wore away and her Ti Bon Ange began to awaken. For the one sense that remains, though it may be faint, is that of hearing. Marie-Aurélie heard through the mists of parting the murmured Miserere and Indulgentiam and de Profundis of the priest, the cry of her mother, the confusion of the house. She heard Rosa's voice as the veil thinned between her and a vast void that only inspired a mindless fear. She had risen and faded and faded further and further. She thought she saw her body lying there, her face wreathed in jasmine. Her past appeared to her like the quick backward movement of a curl of smoke returning to its flame that had just previously burst into life, now unlit, its wick was awaiting the potentiality of light. Not knowing, waiting in the darkness. Knowing nothing.

La Sirène Rosa took her cold hand, it was soft. She would not wake up in the coffin, buried in a grave in Lapeyouse cemetery; neither would she be dragged from it by ghouls who would exhume her in the dead of night to spirit her away down the Main for money, sold into slavery as a zombi. Rosa wet a small white square of cloth with a clear liquid and placed it on Marie-Aurélie's nose and mouth. It contained a dilution of iboga, a herb that produces a mild form of delirium which would serve as a bridge between the terror of the un-dead and the trauma of re-entering the real world. She must be made to be a little out of her mind before she came back.

Marie-Aurélie's funeral service, held at the Cathedral of the Immaculate Conception, was sparsely attended. The ritual of burial at Lapéyrouse cemetery was brief; thunder rolled in the hills of Laventille and rain washed tears and dirt indiscriminately. The grave filled with mud, the flowers in their wreaths, pelted by the downpour, drooped, giving up their fragrance to the unlit gray. The little crowd drifted away, sheltered beneath the bat-like umbrellas, waterlogged. Naza and the ghoul who had carried Antoine Paseau's coffin on his head waited, hidden in the mortuary chapel of the tomb of Louis-Antoine Aimé de la Rochefoucauld, Count of the Holy Roman Empire, for the rain to cease, so as to begin their night's work.

❖　❖　❖

"You ain't hear they hold Naza?" Eliza stood at the bedroom door. Rosa shook her bowed head, she had heard nothing, save Marie-Aurélie's anguish.

"They hold him this morning. Mr. Rât, who does work in the cemetery office, went early, before day-clean. They find him in the hole, he counting seeds; but he can't count more than ten, so he counting, counting, he picking all the seeds from the grain amba feuille in the coffin. Mr. Rât send for the constable, they take him down, but like he gone off his head, they say he snorting like a pig in the cell. He naked, kaka all over him, he can't face the magistrate so they carry him to Sainte-Anne madhouse."

La Sirène Rosa nodded and smiled, "Yes, Liza, he grew up in Sainte-Anne." And thought to herself. "Lalin ka kouwi jis tan jou bawayé." Loosely translated— "The moon runs free, till the sun catches up with it."

Marie-Aurélie had not stirred. "Liza, go to the Cathedral Presbytery and call Father Latour for me, please, Marie must be baptised again. She will be like a child for a long time, then she must go to the country. Nobody must know. Go quick and call him, she coming back. She must see God's face, she must see her God."

"Rosa, Mr. Rât send this."

"Put it by the lamp, go quick now, Liza."

"You not going to read what it say, Rosa?"

"I know what it say, Liza, but go for the priest, go quick."

◆ ◆ ◆

2. Erzulie Freda:-

SÉ KOUTO KI KONNÈT SA KI NAN TCHÈ JONMOU.
It is the knife that knows what is in the heart of the pumpkin.

La Sirène Rosa's grandmother Erzulie Freda was born in Saint-Domingue. There was no date of birth for people like her. For people like her, you were either born before or after the Revolution. Her circumstances were these.

The Count de Molé was already middle-aged when he ventured out to the Antilles. Port-au-Prince afforded him the opportunity to renew his fortune, once a considerable one, which he had squandered in that incurable vice of gambling. Selling off the last of his mother's jewels and a large portion of his ancestral lands in the Auvergne, he invested a sizable sum with the merchants Channand & Fils, who were shippers of slaves and transporters of sugar during the decade and a half before the French Revolution of 1789.

He not only remade his fortune, but was once more in the position to resume the exhilaration of his old affliction. Fortune seemed to smile on all his endeavours. His ships sailed fast. His cards turned with alchemic zeal into gold, and a beautiful African woman quickened his lagging passion and drew him into sensuality and a profound experience of satisfaction. He accommodated Erzulie Freda in his gleaming white mansion, knowing full well that she was the high priestess of a cult dedicated to her own magnificence.

He was witness to the transformations occasioned as a result of her being possessed by the deity of her devotion, which was the goddess of love. He saw with his own eyes the power of the powers that would entrance her, altering her appearance with a terrible beauty. He devoted his energy, his remade fortune and his prestige to her wellbeing, and to the wellbeing of the deity that came to her. He was her most devoted slave.

Upon her ring finger she wore three wedding bands, one for each husband: Damballa, Agwe and Ogoun. Her symbol: the heart; her colours: pink, blue, white and gold; and her favourite sacrifices: jewellery, perfume, sweet cakes and liqueurs.

During the Rada Voudoun ceremonies, he was her serviteur, fetching urgently the soft-scented powders, the silk scarves, the heady perfumes, the zépingue tremblant, the trembling pins of gold, to adorn her magnificent Madras turban.

He held her feet as she sat enthroned, in his lap; she placed upon him the iron chains of slavery, and in so doing enslaved her master.

He would sing the plaintive, long out of fashion love songs of the Auvergne to her, in a high piping voice, and awaken her on a morning to laughter in the happy brilliance of the Eastern-facing bedroom of the great house on the plantation, Averon.

2. ERZULIE FREDA

She was the delight of his present life, his every wish come true. To them was born a beauty, a girl child conceived in the detumescence that follows the derangement of passion, in the fore-day morning that trembled on the brink of dawn, when dew, caught in the art of turning into mists, could only linger but for a moment in the rosy light of a new day.

They called her Ursule Bridgette. She grew in the lap of luxury, running free in the long gallery of his lacy mansion, gay ribbons flying from her red-brown hair. She was a dark-skinned refined featured mulatress, her eyes the deepest green, her little nose upturned, her lips the unopened rose of innocence.

On her 14th birthday, Ursule Bridgette's mother passed away. As the drums rolled and the chorus implored, the Goddess of love descended upon her willing Cheval. Her feet lifted her into the arching flight, the light caught her en-winged as she flew in fierce defiance of her mortality. She had become Maîtresse Erzulie: transcending this omnipresence on to a fresh plateau, courting a pain that contained its own brand of ecstasy. The embodiment of love, the kind of love that inflicts a wound, a gaping hole in which may be glimpsed the crossroads, the cosmic horizontal and vertical place, the point where womankind comes face to face with her immortal, and yes, divine self.

In a dark doorway sat an ugly, deformed boy who looked at Erzulie Freda's smiling beauty with his heart, mind and soul entrapped, these were filled with a sense of hostile enmity, a resentful longing for her possession by that Loa, for her qualities, her beauty and her luck. He wished, and wanted, that he could be her. He loved her, yet hated her. People called him Zinga, because no one knew his name.

Erzulie Freda rose to the brilliance that blazed about her, seeing for a moment all grace and beauty reflected in a face so like her own. As this magnificence bent in shimmering gold to kiss her proffered heart, she fell away, down and around the spiral painted blue, the hissing sound of waves, the salty taste of sea foam, of blood, of tears, with arms outstretched as if crucified on beams of fire. She passed from this world into a blinding difference. Her lover, her serviteur holding her dark face, still familiar, but swiftly turning into death's portal.

◆ ◆ ◆

The seventy-four gun ship-of-the-line, driven by a steady North Easterly breeze of wind, was running rapidly down the Leeward Islands in enormous seas. Above, her vast topsails bellied out, round, taut, packed with the receding remnant of a tropical storm that still pelted huge raindrops which shattered against the wide handrail that he grasped firmly to steady himself, as the great ship shuddered and rose to break free, sending salt spray to mingle with the rain that was running down his cheeks.

"Let's go inside, Papa, I don't want the wind to blow us away." He held Ursule Bridgette close to him. The long hazy line of Saint-Domingue had long since faded. He had not seen the flames that destroyed habitation Averon, nor had he witnessed the uprising, the murder, the destruction, the commencement of the ancestress of all Caribbean Revolutions. The blacks, having remade religion, would now create freedom. Their escape had been providential. Fleeing from the Revolution even before it happened, their journey to the island of Martinique had taken them South along the Caribbean chain of islands, but rumours of war would eventually bring them to the Spanish island of Trinidad.

Amongst the several hundred black and white, slave and free who crowded the careening decks of the battleship "Le Maréchal de Castries" was a dwarfish creature too ugly to be readily recognised as either man or woman. This aberration, this adversary of the certainty that honours woman as the creator of dreams, the Goddess of Love, the muse of perfection, had secretly arranged to be carried aboard, huddled in a seaman's chest that belonged to no one. He, for it was a man, was to be the cutler, sharpening all knives, cutlasses, ploughshares, and scissors on the Coblentz estate, and becoming, over time the plantation's resident Bokor, its Obeah man, loup-garou, shape-changer and poisoner. He, Zinga, had just two possessions: a vial of the most virulent poison to ever leave the island of Saint-Domingue, and the personal knowledge of and experience in a malevolent and profound depravity, the capacity to initiate the most dreaded corruptibility of the human condition in these islands: the creation of the zombi.

3. Ursule Bridgette:-

MALÈ PA KA CHANJÉ KON LAPLI.
Misfortunes do not happen like rain.

"Zèb-mwen-mizé?" she said. "Ès mwen amizé mwen?"
She giggled and poked the T-Marie with her little finger. "Did I amuse myself?" — If the sensitive leaves had
closed shut, it would mean that she had lingered longer
than she should have with Madame Escallière, or had
stopped to look at les blanchisseuses at work with their
washing in the Sainte-Anne river, but they had not. It
was a sure test to discover the truth concerning the an-
tics of playful girls.

"See, Ti-Pap, they do not close, see, see I told you, I
came straight back."

The old slave hid his smile in the folds of his wrinkled
face. Ursule Bridgette was growing like a fine young tree,
Madame Escallière taught her French, a little Spanish,
the mysteries of arithmetic and the art of the Spanish guitar. Ti-Pap taught her Voudoun. Well, that was
an overstatement, he taught her how to maintain the
spirits of her past, honour her ancestresses and something of the secret efficacies of plants and herbs, roots,
barks and bushes. He carved for her, in ebony, a very
pretty little mermaid with long wavy hair a sensuous
tail and somewhat staring eyes, its hands held up, palms

turned towards the little mouth that seemed to be saying "Ooohhaa". He said, "La Sirène will keep you safe from falling to the bottom of the river or even the sea."

Peletan de Molé loved her with his whole heart. Fore-warned by his trusted valet Ti-Pap, they had made their escape from Saint-Domingue soon after the death of her mother, and in so doing managed to escape the calamity of the Revolution. The fortune that he brought to this island was in excess of four thousand Louis d'Or together with a quantity of uncut emeralds from the mines of Spanish Central America, and sixty slaves, forty-seven men and thirteen women. He was a very well-off émigré.

He preferred to keep his slaves, despite the many offers that he received for them. He would house and feed them, and look after them on the property that he acquired in the outskirts of the town of Port-d'Espagne, East of the Dry River bed, from Madame Moncrou, rather than to sell them. They were his people, he knew every one of them, some he had seen come into this world. He put them to work clearing the mangrove on the sea-front side of his property, felling the great silk-cotton trees that covered the foothills of Laventille.

There he would build a jetty at what would be remembered as number twenty nine Port-of-Spain, on the Old St. Joseph Road, and erect an abattoir for slaughtering the wild cattle that he imported from Venezuela. He bought a house from Don Felipe Giovanni Angelo Giorgetti, a Corsican, next to the Catholic Presbytery on the Rue de la Place, called by the English George

Street for their King. Ursule Bridgette had Cyrillia, a girl a little older than herself, and Ti-Pap as her companions. They were amongst four or five domestic slaves who belonged to the household. He had Saint Jacques, an affranchi, a free black man, who drove his carriage and was his body guard.

Boom, boom! "Tonnè, qu'est-ce c'est?" She could remember when they came. Boom -- the English, just in the harbour, boom -- run! Nowhere to run. The harbour fort's cannon is firing away at the British navy, but it is out of range. Boom! Ursule Bridgette saw the foreign soldiers coming into the Calle Principal, the Rue d'Eglise, Nelson Street. The bagpipes made the hair on her arms stand on end.

The island had been taken by the English, the Spaniards putting up no real resistance. The Governor, Don José María Chacón, seemed relieved, slipping away into exile and then into the obscurity of prison. The British super-imposed military law upon the existing medieval Spanish ordinances.

The island teemed with French planters and adventures of all estates who had been pauperised by revolution, war, red ants, the depredations of piracy and by the uprisings of their Negroes. It seethed with plots and conspirators, republicans and anarchists with an eye on down the Main, where a revolution to overthrow the Spanish Crown was being contrived, and as such would offer all manner of rewards.

In 1797, Port-d'Espagne was peopled by half-caste Spaniards, broad-nosed zambos, high-strung mestizo women, French royalists, soldiers, white, black and coloured, semi-retired pirates, a pseudo aristocracy, and the ghosts of conquistadors who had died in the previous centuries in search of El Dorado, eaten by the anthropomorgi people in the jungles of Güiria.

The town's houses were built of thatch and shingles and had mud walls—the Spanish possessed no masonry. There were many Caribs, naked. When they died, and it was always quite suddenly, they were buried in Carib fashion in a small hole, their arms around their knees, all over the place in what is now upper Duncan Street, then known as Calle del Infante, or Rue des Trois Chandelles by the French inhabitants, because of the three candles which were burned on meeting nights at the gate of the Masonic Lodge, Les Frères Unis, whose meeting place was established in 1795 at the corner of Duncan Street and Upper Prince Street, which was in those days called Calle de Santa Rosa.

The voices in the streets shouted in many languages; on any day could be heard the French of the Languedoc, Mandarin Chinese, obscure African languages, Castilian Spanish, public school English, the incomprehensible gibberish of the blacks, Creole Patois, High and Low German, broken English, the Arabic of the Mandingoes, Scottish oaths, Irish lullabies, Carib cuss words, and a Venezuelan twang that would linger on for centuries in the foot hills of the Northern Range.

All this was accompanied by the sounds of hammering, of iron-wheeled traffic, and the clatter of emaciated horses, which served to convey the impression of hectic enterprise. Vile smells rose from the carcasses of animals that were covered by the carrion vultures, and mingled with the rising damp and rot of the mangrove swamp that almost encircled the town, these to combine with those of the public disposal of the contents of chamber pots, coal pot smoke, sawdust, tonka beans rotting, the smell of old women, and the odour of the unwashed.

The slave population of the island, small, stood around fifteen to twenty thousand, give or take the availability of new recruits, births, deaths and those who would maroon themselves in the island's unexplored interior. The plantations were worked frenetically, as the planters sought to capitalise on their investments before the inevitability of the freedom of the blacks became a reality.

The affranchis, the Free Blacks and coloureds, of which they were about ten thousand, hovered on the edges of true liberté, prayed, and said Novenas for divine intervention so as to change their destiny. As a result they projected much vivacity and were given to a pointless pursuit of gaiety. They were perceived as proud, fickle, deceitful, wicked, and capable of the greatest crimes by the béké and by the slaves. The history of the hommes de couleur in all French colonies was the same. Freed from the chain, they were branded mulattoes, mules, half donkey-half horse, becoming, it was said an "Ishmaelitish clan, inimical to both races, and dreaded by both."

On the other hand their sisters, les filles de couleur, were worshipped by the béké as coquettes, prepossessing and beguiling. Some were beautiful beyond imagination, possessing chocolate-brown, café-au-lait, peanut butter or sapodilla complexions, lustrous thick black hair, or frizzy red curls. Seductive with green, blue, black, brown or hazel eyes, their proportions generous and charming, they were remarked upon by the travellers of the day who were confounded by the luxury of their dress and puzzled by the magnificence of their jewellery. All of which was displayed with the air of the triumphant, as they promenaded on the Rue de Sainte-Anne to take the Savannah breeze. They knew how to please, and in a manner unique to themselves, took revenge for the humiliating dependence of their condition by the evocation of the dissolute passions which they excited in their masters, their lovers and the ever-present hopefuls.

It must be said that it was also to the fidelity of their love that these very same masters, on a great many occasions, owed to la fille de couleur the good fortune of having discovered and prevented conspiracies, which would have made them, the owners of the habitations, the easy victims of their slaves. This was why the slaves and the Bokor, the black magic users, hated and envied the beautiful fille de couleur.

For those with an interest in the named variations of these mixed-race beauties, which were dreamed up by the béké, possessed as they were with the idea of keeping their bloodstreams unpolluted by that of the children of Africa; proceeding from dark-skinned to light-skinned: Sacatra, the offspring of a Griffe and a black, seven eighths African blood; Griffe, the offspring of a black and a Mulatto, three quarter African blood; Marabou, the offspring of a Mulatto and a Griffe, five eighths African blood; Mulatto, the offspring of a white and a black, one half African blood; Quadroon, the offspring of a white and a Mulatto, one quarter African blood; Mètif or Octaroon, the offspring of a white and a Quadroon, one eighth African blood; Mamelouque, the offspring of a white and a Mètif, one sixteenth African blood. Then there were the Capresse, a woman of mixed descent, usually Carib and French, with or without some African heritage.

The fifteen hundred or so whites were terrified of the blacks. Those who had known Grenada or Saint-Domingue, knew well the sudden silence that could fall in the heat of the day.

The place was too still, not a bird stirred. It was a silence that could startle you to wakeful watchfulness: the tepid air that filled the room; to turn in your bed, sweat pouring, the still sleeping Négresse at your side, you, stuck in the mosquito net, panic, your nakedness. She grins, you strike it from her face. You stand in the gallery, panting, listening: coming from somewhere is the sound of love-making. That sounds like Luce! My mulatress Luce, somebody is . . . .

The sense of disgust, choking like nausea. In your mind's eye you see the powder fading into the cistern. In the silence of the night you could almost hear the trickle of drops, colourless, tasteless, vanishing into the big goblet on the shady shelf of the Demerara window.

3. URSULE BRIDGETTE

In the far-off distance you hear a léwòz, a solitary ka-drum rapping out a crazy, rapid rhythm, a message. Next morning Mayotte is dead in the kitchen, her madras ka-landé removed from her head, exposing her baldness, her gray chivé tak-tak. The coffee is still hot, throw it out the window, no coffee today. The chien-fer, whim-pering and hairless, still chained to the back steps, did not make one sound.

Those who remembered the events in Grenville, Gre-nada, say it was a Sunday at the start of March 1795, on the Soubise plantation in the Marquis, now Saint An-drew, that a party of persons met and in silence paced the night. The plantation great house shone with an ethereal glow, whiter than white in the full moon. In the gallery, massa and his sons and their wives were rocking gen-tly, digesting, fanning the warm wind. Outside the bwa-kabrit, giant crickets, maintained a shrill staccato that seemed to heat up the night. Those who served them their wine knew well, but kept their faces carefully ar-ranged in servitude, bare feet making whispering sounds on the highly polished floor. Upstairs, in the enormous rooms bathed in a yellow glow, the children slept or stirred or sucked at the huge black breasts of their wet-nurse. She, too, knew. All the slaves of La Bay knew.

The party of persons had slipped from barrack to bar-rack. Their message was their presence. One week later, they struck with a vengeance. A wail of terror destroyed in fire the filigree, the gingerbread and the turned wood of the most beautiful houses in the Caribbean Sea. They butchered all, black, white, and mulatto, including the

English Governor who barred their way. Some stories linger longer, the madness of the slaves, the aristocrats begging for their lives, the perfection of their French theatrical. The body of bloody men surging by, a blond baby spiked through, waving before them as a banner for the damned, their eyes those of the un-dead.

This reality haunted the béké and seemed to follow them from island to island. On Coblentz estate the blacks died with tragic regularity. The cattle died, the dogs, Messieurs de Mallevault and de Montalembert were driven to bankruptcy. In Diego Martin, in Chaguanas, isolated cases of death by poison occurred, were occurring. Monsieur St. Hilaire Bégorrat went to see the Governor, a Colonel Picton. "There is a conspiracy amongst the blacks." He knew. He lived amongst them, sang, danced, and fornicated with them. "Four times in each year the adepts of the society go through a profane and blasphemous ceremony, a parody of the Christian sacrament, when the Grand Judge of the society administers bread and wine. "Remember, the bread you are eating is the white man's flesh; the wine you are drinking is the white man's blood. They all sing; 'Hê Saint-Domingue, remember Saint-Domingue.'" They also sang: "Begorrat et Diabl'la, c'est un; Begorrat et Diabl'la, c'est deux; Begorrat, fort cruel et mauvais; Begorrat roi-la dans son pays."

The authorities moved with unaccustomed alacrity and arrested dozens. The planned outbreak of the slaves, it was believed, was demonstrated by the existence of the secret societies like Les Cochons Sans Poils. Some were home-grown, some imported from the other islands, others were directly out of Africa.

"There is a plan to kill every white on the island, Massa. That is the plan. The machete, the fire."

The two old men sat together in the gallery overlooking the quiet street. One a master, one a slave. They had shared much over the years, they were presently sampling some Armagnac.

"It cannot happen on this island, Ti-Pap. This is a new society you could say, it was invented, what? Twenty years ago, in 1783 with the Cedula of Population. The high feelings are imported from the other islands. And there is not enough blacks. No magic. No power. Just rage and rum."

It is the béké who possess the rage, thought Ti-Pap. And he was right. The memories of the massacres perpetrated by the slaves in Saint-Domingue, Guadeloupe and St. Lucia, just eight or nine years ago, were still fresh. In Grenada, a day's sail away, where the hommes de couleur, Julian Fédon and Stanislas Besson, the slaves, and their Republican 'brigands', had murdered dozens of French families, old women, children, infants taken from the arms of their mothers.

The escaped murderers, people say Fédon himself, and the very close relatives of the murdered, were now refugees all; survivors of those catastrophic events in Grenada, they were now here, living in Trinidad.

Some had come to escape the terror of the night, others to run from the vengeance of the Grenadian authorities. They were living right here, in Port-d'Espagne, several of them almost side by side in the eleven short narrow streets that comprised the town. Some of these French people had relatives, mulatto sons, who were involved with the killings. Somebody said Fédon himself got away; Monsieur Dere from the Franc Maçons helped him to reach Venezuela. Yes. Suspicions seethed, deceit and hate were palpable, revenge, postponed, was on everybody's mind, but it was never forgotten. All this was spat like phlegm, and made into the politics of hate and guilt; it was destined to last for hundreds of years.

The next day on the Plaza de la Marina at the foot of Rue d'Eglise, Nelson Street, a Negro is beheaded: his head sent to St. Joseph and put upon a spike at the entrance of the town. His body, bound to a living man, another conspirator, packed with gun powder and sulphur. They are both set on fire in Brunswick Square.

Peletan de Molé shook his head in dismay.

"No, Ti-Pap, this is not justice, this is vengeance for the past, and in advance of events that may not even take place."

The old slave regarded his master. He is a kind man, he thought, but he don't know African people.

"Massa Peletan, those niggers bad, too bad, the Gob'na do the right thing, you have to strike off the head, crush it good, then throw it in the fire, even then it not dead enough."

"The revenge for this will go underground, Ti-Pap, you know that, and will surface in the most unexpected places."

The revenge is going on all the time, thought Ti-Pap, the real revenge we take out upon ourselves, then on each other. He don't know how it feels to know that is people like yourself who turn round and sell you to the ship. He don't know how you feel as you go, you look back, and see them there, they not looking back, they going home to do their business. You gone to hell. Gone forever. That is the first betrayal, the root of the madness.

"Try a little Armagnac, my dear Ti-Pap do not be downcast, it is good for old age, the label reads: 'It makes disappear redness and burning of the eyes; it cures hepatitis, it cures gout, cankers, and fistula by ingestion; restores the paralysed member by massage.' You hear that, Ti-Pap, that's for us. 'It heals wounds of the skin by application. It enlivens the spirit, partaken in moderation, recalls the past to memory, renders men joyous, preserves youth and retards senility.' All this we need! 'And when retained in the mouth, it loosens the tongue and emboldens the wit, if someone timid from time to time himself permits.' Ahh good stuff, Armagnac."

The French planters knew about poison, and poisoners. So did the Corsican tradesmen. Poison, the scandal of the poisoners of Paris during a previous reign, the black Masses said by defrocked priests on the bodies of living naked beauties, names written on paper and passed beneath the chalice, black magic, shocked and terrified the capital. All this travelled to these islands where the life on the plantations, the isolation, the uncertainty, produced an intimacy in the lives of the whites and the blacks. Subtle, syncretic and complicated. The witch-craft of Europe met and mingled with the magic of Africa.

Either the estate held a poisoner or it did not. The most commonly used poison was of course arsenic. It was used in the fields as an insecticide. But there were other sinister poisons such as the venom of snakes, centipedes, scorpions, the pulpy white starch that oozed from the manchineel plant. The dirt from graves and cesspits was easy to obtain, so too ground glass, as well as many roots and herbs. Datura or concombre zombi, slyly administered, would cause hallucinations, people around you would think you going mad, and you would be put away. Some poisons would mean instant death, or on the other hand, the wasting illnesses that could turn a person into a yellow bag of bones. Of spells, there were several; the coup l'aire, an air spell, which was administered by the Bokor's breath and could stop speech; the kou nam, a soul spell, which was a means of capturing the Ti Bon Ange of an individual; and the coup poudre, a magical powder that could cause illness or death. The poisoners, the ones who held real power, the power of life or death in their hands on the estates, did go underground. They struck at the soft underbelly of the plantation: the stupid, the drunken, the children, the indiscrete, the lazy, the women.

"Where is the boy, you stupid woman! Where is my son?"

"I eh no Massa, the dwen take him, Oh Gawd, Oh Gawd Oh."

3. URSULE BRIDGETTE

Poison was used to fight slavery by men of power. "No children born in chains" and the slave women would not breed. "Fire in the mountain" and a handsome harvest would vanish in hot air. "No strength to slavery" and the Zebu bull would fall, the yoke broken. In such a manner they thwarted the profitability of unjust gains. Death was a viable alternative to a life of bondage, and was sought after to gain release. To go home.

The fear of being buried alive gripped everyone, the fear of being given a potion that showed death-like symptoms, to awaken in the closed-in pitch-black airlessness of a coffin six feet underground. Everyone, black or white, knew that was the ultimate revenge. To be made dead, but to be un-dead, to be taken from the grave and shipped out to wander in a strange land. Even if you came back home, people would run like hell if they saw you, they would think that they were seeing your ghost, or spirits, or Jumbies. That was the ultimate sentence, the absolute revenge.

That sentence was applied when profound injustice with no hope of retribution was dished out between the enslaved themselves, and for vengeance, too, it was sought, at a price, when a master, too cruel to accommodate, had to be got rid of. Or for money. Poison was used by an old man gone mad, with an old man's sense of obsolescence, in a place so far from his ancestral home that it might just as well be hell. Seventy slaves died at Coblentz estate in nine months in the year 1803, and murder and evil haunted the nearby plantation of Hollandais, whose great house was named La Fantaisie.

Amongst those who lived to tell the tale was an incredibly ugly man and a beautiful mulatress. He, you have met. She was my grandmother's grandmother, Eugenie Amélie Roussillac.

◆ ◆ ◆

Ursule Bridgette de Molé inherited a small fortune upon the death of her father Peletan, Count de Molé.

"Your father leave this for you, ma chè."

Ti-Pap sat opposite to her in the drawing room of the George Street house. On the round white wicker side table was a small iron chest.

"Open it."

"Oh, Ti-Pap, what is in it?"

"It is gold, Ursule, Louis d'Or, more of them than I can count. But look well, there is more."

Peletan de Molé remade his fortune in Saint-Domingue and had been able to retain it despite his inclinations to ride the wings of chance. In Port-d'Espagne his life had been simple, he had not invested in the great estates, he did not possess hundreds of acres of waving cane, neither did he seek the manpower to work it. As such he escaped the vicissitudes of that volatile industry. Instead he provided beef, steaks for the American sailors, roast for the British and bones full of marrow to nourish the poor. Fine leather came from his hides to beat upon the pavements of the little town.

3. URSULE BRIDGETTE

His wealth lay in the remnant of his fortune in gold coins that he had brought with him, much less than half the original amount, and the properties that he acquired in the town. A careful man he became in his old age. All his papers were in order. His will, in which he left all his worldly goods to Ursule Bridgette, freedom to Ti-Pap, Cyrillia and a dozen others, the remnant of his original slaves, each to receive modest sums so as to enable them a start in life or end it well, now that they were all old, had been witnessed and registered. In the iron box were the title deeds to his properties in Saint-Domingue and here in Trinidad.

"And for you there is this as well."

Ti-Pap drew from under his chair the Govi, a clay pot of African make, its lid made fast and sealed. "This is your heritage, as a black, it is the dwelling place of the voices of the Loa, the deities. Massa Peletan was a Massa, a béké, but he was a serviteur of the Loa that came to your Mama, his soul too must be rescued from the waters under the earth. In one year and one day."

"Oh Ti-Pap, is there anyone on this island to manage such a thing?"

"Oui, ma chè, amongst our people and others who came from Saint-Domingue there are Hougan and Mambo who have the power so summon les Invisibles, the souls of the departed, to come and so speak on behalf of your dead Papa. But think not of this now, there is time enough. The gold is a secret, ma chè, come, I will show you where it is kept."

Ursule Bridgette followed Ti-Pap into her father's bedroom. It held the huge old bed that she knew so well, a few elegant Louis Quinze arm-chairs, a large mahogany desk with brass castors, an elegantly made mahogany wardrobe, a seaman's chest, an almost life-sized oil painting of his Mama framed in gold-leaf, a wash-stand, his things, a basin and ewer in heavy silver, and a beautifully made, heart-shaped silver rococo jewellery box with the initials of the Emperor Napoleon and the Empress Josephine inlaid in gold, a trophy from the time when he was possessed by the vice of gambling, his gold seal ring, books, other things that still carried his familiar smells, the evidence of his final illness, details of his life's story. The old man walked towards the bed and pressed firmly on one of the carvings and a panel at the base of the big bedpost swung open to reveal a small cupboard just big enough to conceal the iron box.

"There," he said, and smiled at her astonishment.

◆　◆　◆

Theirs was the only house on the Rue de la Place that was not destroyed by the great conflagration of 1808 that saw the end of the original Spanish town. Ursule Bridgette commenced her astonishing career first as a healer; then as a dispenser of charity and an accommodator of the distressed, of which there were legion. Her kitchen never stopped cooking. The ground floor of her house smelled and looked like an hospital.

Owner-less slaves, abandoned in the helplessness of old age or infirmity, lost souls, the temporarily insane, the poor, the hopeless found her and received some form of comfort.

Like a Florence Nightingale she moved amongst them, lamp in hand, Ti-Pap trailing in her wake with a bucket of cow heel soup. At a young age she became something of a celebrity; people stepped aside to let her pass when she went to church at the newly built Cathedral of the Immaculate Conception.

Ursule Bridgette de Molé, godmother of hundreds, patroness of the homeless, feeder of the hungry. Donations to her efforts would appear. Guinée hens scratched in her yard, morocoys moved with prehistoric slow-motion in her garden, and bags of crabs arrived from unknown donors. Sometimes there was cash, a little bundle of old Spanish silver coins tied up in a red rag. A bright golden British Guinea struck with an elephant, a reminder of the origin of the gold, from a Mandingo Muhammadan whose leg she had saved from amputation.

The Catholic church officials, incapable of telling the difference between the pure religion which she practiced and its ancient enemy, the work of the deceiver, were wary of her; they believed instinctively that she was a witch who cured by touch, administered herbal remedies and invoked the heathen gods and goddesses of Africa in trance-like states as she swirled and stamped and danced and sang in her high-pitched voice while assuming the terrible beauty of her long-dead ancestress. The authorities, alarmed, began to pay attention to her: her following was too big, her influence was growing with the ordinary people and the affranchi blacks and free-coloureds; even the béké, who, accustomed by their faith to the miraculous and naturally superstitious by instinct and temperament, saw in her a living saint.

Ursule Bridgette moved her festivities and feast-days further up and into the Laventille hills than most people would venture, into a natural amphitheatre with a spring at its centre that was surrounded by enormous sandbox and silk-cotton trees. There on nights beneath a rising full moon, after the mangé Guinée, the ritual feeding, the drums would roll and the Loa of Erzulie Freda would be evoked; her serviteurs, moved with the passion of their possession, together with Ursule Bridgette, would dance the Banda, a suggestive dance, to the battérie-maçonnique of small bula drums, beaten swiftly, accompanied by the clapping of hands, at the request of a Loa, sometimes Ghede, who having mounted a head, would feel like doing a gay dance for a displaced people that remembered the divinities of their homeland.

That her religious practices challenged the orthodoxy of established miracle-makers of both the black and the white variety, was a certainty. The white went to the police, to the government, surely there were laws against Obeah, black magic, taking money under false pretense. The black tended to take things personally.

Ursule Bridgette's hands were clean, her religion, brought to Trinidad from Saint-Domingue in the 1780s where it was called Vodoun, was to become known as Shango here, and was in essence based on the metaphysical principles and the rituals practiced by West African peoples for millennia. Renewed and readapted in our experience of slavery in the New World it was syncretic in character. It remained strongly influenced by Dahomean beliefs and cults, amongst others, but it was also shaped by the dominant Roman Catholic religious beliefs in which it existed. It was in fact the opposite of Obeah, with which it had arrived here almost simultaneously. Obeah dealt in poisons, trickery and sorcery and was the companion of murder, and could ultimately end with lunacy, as we shall see.

No one came to testify against her, there was no evidence except the gratitude for her kindnesses. There were others who envied her and saw themselves in conflict with her, they wished to get and keep control of all that was called the djamèt culture, the Afro Creole masses, the ones who lived beyond the perimeter of polite society. These were the evil sorcerers who would break her, if they could.

◆ ◆ ◆

The old poisoner of Coblentz estate, they called him Zinga, now inhabited the abandoned slave barracks up Rue La Fantaisie, which led to one of the three plantations that nestled in the foothills of the Sainte-Anne valley. He made his shrine in the abandoned graveyard of the estate, where the unmarked graves of his forgotten victims gave nourishment to the moss-hung samaan trees: all lending to the place an absolutely melancholy and damp atmosphere. Living, at times secretly, in the depths of the crypt of the Baron Ignacio de Mallevault's tomb, which once contained a consecrated mortuary chapel dedicated to de Mallevault's patron saint, Saint Ignacio López de Loyola, the old man made use of the Baron's disembodied skull-box as an apothecary's mortar for the poisonous potions concocted by him, and, from time to time, as a washbasin. He had as boon companions a seventeen-foot anaconda and a female mapapire zanana. The disporting of himself with these enemies of the people, both in his public appearances and in private audiences, readily conveyed the idea of his deadly power to his specially selected customers. The Spanish spy Domingo Vallecilla, for example, came to procure a poison—to change the course of history, he claimed, while farting in fear in his pantaloons.

The boy who attached himself to him was, unbeknownst to either of them, his own son, sent by his mother to Zinga before her death. The boy became the old poisoner's grateful servant and willing accomplice. The boy's fear, his fear from almost infancy, had been born in the circumstances of his birth. His mother, Desirée Bouga, one could say, was a daemon in her own right; she was a soukounyan who ran a school for the graduation of her kind and was once the terror of Morne Repos, Casa Blanca and the other hillside villages of Hololo and the upper Cascade valley, from the 1800s.

Desirée Bouga's demise had been as the result of a curse, the curse of counting. This had been put upon her by the last of the Spanish priests to the Mission of Ariapita. Drawing from the Grimoire of Armabal the Moor, Padre Pedro Paulo Sa Avadré condemned her and her offspring to pick up and count, before the rising of the sun, any amount of grains, be they seed, rice or corn, that was laid before them during the act that they had committed for the benefit of the evil powers which they served and to whom they had obligated their immortal souls. Padre Pedro Paulo Sa Avadré offered to The Lord Most High "The Prayer to Saint Michael" to give him strength of will and firm conviction in his faith. "Sancte Michael Archangele, defende nos in proelio; contra nequitiam et insidias diaboli esto praesidium. Imperet illi Deus, supplices deprecamur: tuque, Princeps militiae Caelestis, satanam aliosque spiritus malignos, qui ad perditionem animarum pervagantur in mundo, divina virtute in infernum detrude. Amen."

In the beginning the boy, who at first had no name, was treated by the old poisoner like a dog. He was chained to the gate, beaten, compelled to walk on all fours, taught how to bark and encouraged to bite. The boy became the old poisoner's menial servant, his apprentice, and over time the vehicle for his intentions. The boy, who would come to be known as Naza, started his career as the provider of Bufo marinus, the Goliath frog, Conraua Goliath, alias big crapaud, for the old Obeahman, from which they extracted the rot-making poisons that could turn a mere scratch into a sore that could cost a leg or a life, or make a potential witness lose his voice in the Courthouse in Town by the application of a coup l'aire.

Naza acquired a knowledge of spiders, of knowing the ones that delivered the most poisonous venoms, and the use of intoxicants, narcotics and hallucinogens. He also acquired the knowledge of antidotes, vital to his forthcoming career as poisoner and Obeahman. The boy was not allowed to handle the oddly-shaped thunder-stone that rested on the desecrated altar of the Baron's mortuary chapel. This was regarded as sacred, as it had been forged by Sobo and Shango who were the spirits of lightning and thunder, and had come to the old man's hand after a bolt of lightning had struck a boulder on the summit of Mount Mal-d'Estomac, striking off a segment. This had lain for one year and a day before it could be handled by the practitioner.

Now almost a cripple, the old man was convinced that he had his successor, who, if he were to receive the final initiation, must commit the ultimate act. In the darkness of the crypt the old man struck a match, to commence the Canzo, the ordeal by fire to initiate the boy Naza into the art of Les Cochons Sans Poils. As the wavering shadows leapt up the peeling walls, an old enamelled chamberpot burst into flames. Without a moment's hesitation Zinga plunged his hands into them, and with his hands ablaze he passed the fire to the boy's hands, then cuffed him about his head, shoulders and body. Before them was a jar, in it was the remains of a great toad to which had been attached by a pin a scorpion. The bite of the insect caused the toad to secrete forty-five potent, deadly chemicals from glands on the back of its head. Suspended in the liquid was a plant called pois gratter, a macuna, the itching plant. On its seeds were tiny hairs that had the effect of causing a person who came into contact with them to experience red hot needles entering their flesh. The boy, now an engagé, his pact made, was bound to fulfil the exacting obligation that was given to him by the old Obeah man, Zinga.

". . . and as a reward you will have all this."

◆　◆　◆

Louis Rémy had sailed from the Port of Marseille in 1798 aboard his own ship, the Jon Zac, the terror of 'the Terror' fresh in his mind. Because of the Revolution, he, like tens of thousands of French people, left for the New World in pursuit of a novel and more marvellous life. He brought to Trinidad his wife, three daughters and his considerable fortune. He acquired a town house on lower Henry Street, which was called by the French inhabitants Rue Neuve and remembered by the old Spanish people as Calle Herrera. He established a warehouse on the Plaza de la Marina and hired two impoverished German immigrants as clerks.

He wore pastel-coloured silk shirts in the stifling heat of the tropical day without perspiring, carried a rapier with a ruby set into a golden shell on its hilt, sported the going-out-of-style plus fours of dark green velvet, with cream hose, black patent leather shoes with silver buckles, and tied his long black hair with a thin red velvet ribbon.

He caught her eye in the noisy Charlotte Street market. For a fleeting moment they stared at each other. To her, he seemed quixotic, his sharp blue eyes, Frida Kahlo eyebrows, long thin nose, obvious ears and quick movements made her think of some wild, unknown unpropitious bird from an undiscovered continent. To him, she appeared as out of a long story told by a traveller who had lost his way in a period of time unsuspected, in a place anticipated only in half-remembered daydreams.

Ursule Bridgette was dressed in a white lacy costume, a donation from a retired courtesan who had caused a now forgotten sensation at the court of Louis XVI in the last anguished moments of the ancien régime, and who presently resided, in reduced circumstances, on Piccadilly Street in one of those tiny gingerbread houses that have miraculously survived to the twenty-first century.

She had kept the lacy dress for herself because of the pastoral air that it conveyed, which allowed her to pretend, when she carried a miniature magenta parasol, that she was a shepherdess. With it she wore an enormously tall, hand-painted black and yellow plaid madras turban, upon which was perched an absurdly small straw hat. A collier-chou, a gorgeous necklace that comprised several rows of large hollow gold beads, wrapped several times around her slender neck, this was matched by a pair of enormous gold earrings which accentuated the thick golden bracelets with their big cocoa pod rondels.

3. URSULE BRIDGETTE

He noted that everywhere she went, the people smiled and spoke kindly and sought to touch her slim hand, her hem, her shoulder. She would turn and smile a dazzling smile. Her topaz eyes, her gazelle legs, her slender neck, delicate collar bones, her high round dancer's bottom, her little girl breasts, her café-un-peu-au-lait complexion, caused a breathlessness that took him by surprise, particularly when he noticed that he had sweated through his pistachio-coloured Persian silk shirt.

She stayed long in the market, admiring the blue and red macaws, the inquisitive toucans and the charming Sisserou parrots from Dominica, while avoiding the co-matose iguanas, their legs tied up behind their backs with vines forming handles, to facilitate their easy car-riage; inhaling the innervating salt air emanating from the vast quantities of silver moonshine fish, carite, cro-cro and king; enjoying the aromas of the heaps of funi-ty, the fragrant chive, rosemary and Spanish thyme of Paramin, the heaps of cloves and spice, the pyramids of cinnamon, prickly red roucou, the immortal cascadura, waiting to make foreigners into Trinidadians.

All turned their heads to see them trailing along, fol-lowing each other, getting lost, finding each other be-hind bags of yam, piles of cassava, mountains of callaloo bush, trays of okras, slabs of pork, bundles of clean-neck chickens, frizzle fowls in assorted colours, fierce yellow-eyed fighting cocks smelling of rum, haunches of turtle still alive and twitching, eggs attached, cobweb and co-coyea-brooms and demijohns of molasses and rum.

He wrote her poems in the style of the troubadours in perfect Provençal, and sent to her petals of white lilies where he inscribed with pin pricks an intimation of his urgent desire.

She was entranced, became confused and made a misguided attempt to dress better for him, forcing her naturally wide feet into tiny Croatian slippers. She experimented without success with French underwear, imported perfumes and scented fans from St. Lucia, applied temporary beauty marks to inappropriate places, and modeled dominoes with very little else on, to the amazement of her tomcat who stalked from her bedroom in disgust.

She tried fascinator veils with tiny black polka-dots and manteaus with elaborate combs made from the shell of ocean-going turtles that had commenced their mysterious voyages when the Admiral of the Ocean Sea was but a boy in Genoa.

He sang in a clear and boyish soprano beneath her window in the dead of night, to the amusement of the vagrants, startling the Guinée fowl and geese that kept vigil against Obeah in her front yard to raucous responses, which was immediately joined by the howls of the lachrymose stray dogs and the wails of sentimental felines. She let him in to save herself from the embarrassment of becoming the topic of one of next year's calypsos.

Caught in the surprise of the immediacy of their longing, their first attempt at conversation was similar to the phenomenon of speaking in tongues, but when she accidentally touched his arm he immediately knocked over the Louis XIV crystal decanter that belonged to her father and which she deftly caught; thus, they both fell to kissing in relief that the distraction had caused. She tasted of cloves, he, of cognac, she was taller, he stood on tip-toes to gain a purchase on her lips, her eyes, her cheekbones, she released his hair by pulling on the red velvet bow, sending it cascading about his pale blue silk shirt. They both sank to the hard pitch pine floor, endeavouring to overcome the absurdities of early nineteenth century dress codes so as to find each other.

He was neither surprised nor alarmed by her hallucinogenic lifestyle, nor was she put out by the minuet-like clockwork of his. But they synchronised their goings and comings, mutual and simultaneous orgasms, their accumulation of wealth, their seasicknesses and their health, literally until death took him away twenty-three years later, bringing an end to their loving plaçage. She bore him one daughter whose name was La Sirène Rosa Rémy.

◆　◆　◆

4. Eugénie Amélie:-

SÉ LÈ VAN KA VANTÉ, MOUN KA WÈ LAPO POUL.
It is when the wind is blowing that we see the skin of the fowl.

My grandmother's grandmother, whose name was Eugénie Amélie Roussillac, was born on the island of Dominica in the last anguished years of the eighteenth century when it appeared to thinking people that the world was coming to an end. Her father, it was said, was a Frenchman from Nice, a butcher by profession, who had been sentenced to five years deportation for the attempted murder of a cooper, over a matter of honour. It would appear that he had attempted to drown the man in a barrel of his own manufacture. For five years he laboured in the cane fields alongside the seventeen African slaves and three Canary islanders who, like himself, were indentured to Clotilde Monvoisin. Freed from indentureship, his life forever altered, he practiced his profession at the gran' market in Roseau.

As soon as he had enough money put by, he presented himself at the slave market at the harbour frontage, and for the sum of one hundred and eighty silver pilar—Mexican-Spanish dollars, he bought a tall, flat-chested, aggressive Ibo woman to be his housekeeper, companion and mistress. His choice was inspired by the fact that the available white women on the island of his class were absolutely worn out by their previous profession of prostitution and experience of poverty in France, followed by five years of working under the tropical sun.

Much in this manner, in those days there came into being three classes, the white, the mulatto and the black, which at that time implied no particular evil, except the obvious one of slavery.

Their domestic life together, as it was remembered by those who were not present, was organised along the lines of never-ending attack, defence, capitulation, occupation, revolt and overthrow; which was followed by accommodation and the perpetual destruction of most of their worldly goods.

It was during one of their more ferocious engagements that Eugénie Amélie Roussillac was conceived. This momentous event coincided with the eye of the most devastating hurricane ever to surge out of the Atlantic Ocean staring down upon the blasted mountainsides of Morne Trois Pitons, flinging flocks of Sisserou parrots into hysterics, and turning the waters of the Boiling Lake into a turbulent cauldron of hissing rising steam: that was the moment when her Papa, having achieved a momentary purchase, was again overthrown from his situation and to the floor by the side of the bed in their small house that was clinging precariously to the sides of that devastated mountain.

As a consequence, there was no more offspring to the state of war that passed for their relationship. After a while, he forgot that he owned her and she, despising both her keeper and their offspring, became a wealthy marchande in control of her own macoute that contained not only proceeds of her day's sales but a long sharp dagger imported from Guadalajara.

My grandmother's grandmother, Eugénie Amélie, as it was related to me by my gran Tanti Phillippa, grew to possess her mother's height, but not her temperament, her father's commitment to survival, but not his lack of ambition. She belonged to a category of persons who were woven into the very fabric of the island's society. She belonged to all classes and to none.

For the fille de couleur there was one way in which to conquer: Eugénie, fortunate with her youthful, natural naiveté that was combined with a touching gracefulness, possessed about her an incipient allure that could be glimpsed at times in the lascivious languor of her smile, and the rise of her bonda, this she had also inherited from her mother, a beautiful black woman's backside. These charms, at that time unappreciated by her, were a potent combination, one that could inflame the most placid, the most disdainful or the most sanctimonious of men.

The island was too small. There was too much competition. She needed a more cosmopolitan environment. She found passage on a windjammer when hardly seventeen by charging her favourite currency and a day later arrived on the beautiful island of Martinique. She, within a week of her arrival in Fort-de-France, became the plaything of a retired Spanish Admiral who owned a plantation on nearby Les Trois-Îlets.

Legend has it that he was attempting to paint, in watercolour, on my grandmother's grandmother's smooth, slightly palpitating stomach, his interpretation of the famous Battle of Cape Passero, which saw the defeat of an entire Spanish fleet under Admirals Antonio de Gaztañeta and Fernando Chacón by a British fleet under Admiral George Byng, near Cape Passero, Sicily, on 11 August 1718, when the calamity of revolution overwhelmed them.

Their escape, as described by his later biographers, was propitious. For propriety's sake she was written out of the story. Fleeing from and in fear of the republican terrorist Victor Hugues, they embarked on a swift schooner sailing for the islands "de barlovento," to the Windward, and arrived in Spanish Trinidad in time to enjoy the petit carême.

The journey, or perhaps the exertions occasioned by his longings, was to prove too much for this old salt, but, before death closed his eyes, he provided for her by introducing her, and recommending her as housekeeper, companion and friend to his young protégé, Jean Éli Maximilien, Baron de Montalembert. He himself had recently escaped the guillotine during a period of a particularly bloody war of retribution conducted with legendary savagery by all concerned by immigrating to Trinidad, where he had been joined by another young aristocrat by the name of Baron Ignacio de Mallevault in an agricultural enterprise in the Sainte-Anne valley at a site where two rivers met. They called this habitation for sentimental reasons, Coblentz.

In the days of great peace, their loving plaçage pro-duced a boy of exceptional beauty and natural intelli-gence. He was his father's constant companion and ac-quired from him a courtly charm that would serve him over the years of his long life in good stead.

The circumstances of the failure of the enterprise at the habitation Coblentz has been intimated above; it was the work, as we have seen, of an evil that resided in the heart of the plantation. It was also a casualty of the time when young men, driven to remake their fortunes in the calamitous period brought about by the French Revolution, were the victims of greed.

The young man, who was fortunate to escape the tragedies of that place, was named for his grandfather, Pierre Éli Xavier Maximilien, and was sent to France for his education from an early age. There he acquaint-ed himself with his father's people and was accepted as a member of this old and distinguished family. He studied medicine at the University of Montpellier in the Languedoc-Roussillon, where his ancestors in times long past had put down their roots; there he met, and was fortunate to marry, Marie Céleste Henriette Victo-rine Étampes de Maguelonne.

They returned to Trinidad and he established a medi-cal practice in Port-d'Espagne on the Rue des Anglais, which was also called Frederick Street in honour of the Prince Regent, son of the mad King George III, and bought a property on the Sainte-Anne road less than quarter of a mile up from Rue La Fantaisie.

4. EUGÉNIE AMÉLIE

They were blessed with seven boys and five girls, all of whom lived, praise God; the eldest of the girls, their second child, was my grandmother, named for hers, Eugénie Amélie, she and La Sirène Rosa Rémy would become drawn together by love and the strange faculty that came to my grandmother early in her youth. She was a natural femme-dormeuse. A person gifted with the ability to communicate with saints and spirits and to see into the future from behind her closed eyes during a séance.

◆　◆　◆

5. La Sirène Rosa:-

*TAN MOUN KONNÈT LÒT NAN GWANJOU, NAN NWIT YO
PA BIZWEN CHANDÈL POU KLÉWÈ YO.*
*When a person has known another in the day-time, he does not need
a candle to recognise him in at night.*

The emancipation of the slaves in the British Empire on the 1st of August 1834 was greeted with jubilation. In the streets of Port-d'Espagne the people danced and sang French ariettes oubliées. Some, with mock solemnity, but with strong emotions, buried in the public squares and in private places the iron chains, shackles and iron balls that were synonymous with slavery, others burned or tore to pieces those certificates called "free-papers" that declared them to be free people. A great quantity simply left where they were to find work in other places, while some with no understanding of what had transpired and fearful of the unknown condition that was called freedom, begged their former owners not to disown them.

When it was understood that they were to serve six more years there was consternation. "Pas de six ans," they wept. "Point de six ans. Pas de six, nous ne voulons pas de six ans, nous sommes libres, le Roi nous a donné la liberté." It seemed to them inconceivable, unconscionable to give something so precious and then to deny its actuality. In a peculiar way this duplicity would characterise their future for generations. But, for the moment, bottles of warap made the rounds, rum sweet rum, fire in the bellies of the free, laughter, the shouts of "Videz les lieux!. . . ." Get out! Leave the property, go free!

La Sirène Rosa, her mother Ursule Bridgette and Ti-Pap sat in the gallery of the house on the Rue de la Place, now increasingly called by the people of the town, George Street. They watched the festivities, joyous, in spite of what was suspected to be the mischief of the békés, the planters and the British merchants of the Town.

"Six more years, Ti-Pap. You think that can be enforced, endured?" He merely smiled, and shook his head. 'Wavèt pa jamen tini wézon douvan poul,' he thought.

"What is happenin, Mama, why is Ti-Pap thinking cock-a-roach must be careful with chickens, eh Mama, will you have to cobweb and sweep, wash all the clothes, go to the market and clean out Cocotte and Lorite's cage, eh Mama?"

"Perhaps, chè moin, yon dwa paka pwan pis, I am sure that you will help me, you are a very good sweeper."

"No, no Mama, I am occupied these days, and Cocotte is too bad, she wants to bite me all the time, and as for naughty Lorite, he will fly away."

"Then maybe you could help me with the cooking, what you think, eh?"

Little Rosa struck a pose that she thought conveyed anxious preoccupation, and busied herself with her new Martiniquian doll.

"So, Ti-Pap," said Ursule Bridgette, closing a silver, heart-shaped jewellery box in which she kept her notions, and turning to him. "Freedom is given at last to the children born in chains, it is a miracle. I never felt that the béké would relinquish his hold on free labour. Is it abandonment, you think, will they now leave these islands, give them over to them?" She gestured, with her lips and a slight up-tilt of her head, to the throngs of dancing, laughing, black people who filled the street below them.

"Ah ma chè, freedom is a thing not so readily received, in truth, it must not be given at all. Freedom dished out in a speech by the Gob'na cannot free the mind, or give liberty to the soul. These poor blacks know nothing. The majority of them you see there were born in Ti Guinée, day before yesterday, all they know is Massa, freedom is given, but Massa will rule, not them."

"Yes, I know what you mean, freedom should be won, should be fought and sacrificed for, like the blacks did in Saint-Domingue, it must be wrested away from they who keep you from it, for it to be true."

"For it to be appreciated, not so?"

"Quite so, Ti-Pap, but it's here, now. We have eleven slaves, three in the house and eight at the abattoir, they will now have to receive money for the work they do, we must now hire a different manager, one who can write and figure things out. I must speak to Louis, he may be able to find a person for us."

At the mention of her father's name, La Sirène Rosa was all ears and big round hazel eyes.

"Is my Papa coming now, tonight, Mama, is he coming to see us, Mama?"

"No darling, he is coming in the morning, we are going to La Montserrat for a week to see Popota and La Belle Tété, would you like to come?"

"Yes, Mama oh yes, yes." She stood on tiptoe and for a moment looked for all the world like the image of her father. "Ti-Pap, Ti-Pap, are you coming too? I want you to show me how ride on Popota, you have to hold him for me." "Not this time, ma chè, next time, Papa will hold him for you, I have to go to and see to the other animals."

"The mad bulls, Ti-Pap?"

"Yes, the mad bulls, bonnwit, ma chè. Bonnwit, Ursule, tomorrow is another day."

The now quite old man rose a little unsteadily, reached for his pipe and antique hat, took his stick from the corner of the gallery, bowed a little bow, and left them sitting, looking out at the festivities.

He did indeed notice the Marianne-lapo-figue dancing, coming towards him, and shifted to one side on the narrow pavement to allow the cow-horned figure dressed in dried banana leaves to pass by. For a moment he did notice that it was a boy, an ugly boy playing the part of a woman, dancing in a mincing manner that suggested fornication, aggressive and obscene. The flickering lights of the flambeaus, the black faces, gaping mouths, rolling eyes. Confusion, noise, he turned into the gateway that led to his little house, not noticing that the dancing figure had gone before him.

"What you want there boy?" he shouted, the figure had startled him. "What you doing there? Get out, before I buss your skin!" The figure, no longer stooping, rose and ran towards to the back of the compound towards the Savane Ceduine, laughing as it fled, laughing, laughing.

"Ah Caramba! Damn fool!"

His next step brought instant agony to his bare left foot and almost instantly to the right one. He knew immediately what had happened to him, the boy was a Pwin, the evil agent of a Bokor, an Obeahman, and what entered his flesh was a poison. He sat down heavily in the darkness on the dirt, his legs stretched out before him, already the pain had achieved a fresh velocity as waves of agony filled his entire being. It occurred to him that he was going to die. The slivers of hard pointed bamboo had penetrated the thick soles of feet that had never known a pair of shoes, delivering the noxious cocktail of poisons enhanced by the tiny hairs of the macuna plant. They would not only kill him, they wanted him to die in agony. He peed where he sat.

"Ahhh, Papa Legba." He sighed, trying to accustom himself to the pain. "We meet at the gate . . . Open the road for me please, do not let any evil spirits bar my path, you are the boss of time, time to go home. . .Ahhh Massa Ghede, the cross-roads face me . . ." He leaned over on his side, a spasm shook him, the poison had entered his blood stream. He sang hoarsely "After God we are in your hands, Ghede Nimbo . . . Ghede Nimbo . . . keeper of the cemetery, overseer of the past, recorder of my heritage and my race . . .Ahhh ai, ai, ai, ai, aiiiii . . . Ghede Nimbo, I am beneath you, Ghede; . . . I am distressed. I no longer labour, weed, and carry, regardez le Baron Samedi . . . now we go home . . . Ti Guinée, at last." The poison had entered his heart. He dreamed— "I adore, I adore her, I revere her, she cherishes me. What does that mean? "ADORATION," a beautiful chorus sang.

Ti-Pap had been a devout Roman Catholic. To his understanding, the real purpose of this elaborately-told myth was to explain the introduction of Love to this world, especially to the béké. He was much involved with the Cathedral, he swept its fore-court religiously whenever he attended High Mass, in much the same manner that he swept his own peristyle on ceremonial occasions. He never, however, allowed his belief in Christianity to interfere with his obligations or his allegiance to the Orisha faith. For him, the Supreme One, whether called Olorun, Yahwe, or Chukwa Asko, was the Grand Maître, all one and the same creator, known and recognised by all. Especially as he became older, he knew the Supreme One, the Great Spirit, reveals itself to various men in various ways. There was no conflict.

La Sirène Rosa could remember Ti-Pap's wake, although she was just five or six when he died. She had a

clear mental picture of his compound that he had cre-
ated on the small parcel of land given to him by the old
Count at the foot of Calvary Hill and Arnold Street, later
known as Piccadilly Street. She could plainly recall the
Hounfour and the acolytes who served there, the cala-
bashes floating in tubs of water, beaten by the old men
with long baguettes, sticks turned down on the end, in
Ti-Pap's old peristyle, roofed with tirite, where the ceremonies took place. The former slaves who came to take
turns on the assator drums for Damballah Wedo and for
Ayida Wedo and for Shango, and who were mounted
by the Loa of the drum, and the lovely children whose
sweet voices sang the Retirer d'en bas de l'eau, the rites
of reclamation of his Gros Bon Ange. She could remember clearly the tall girl with a large açon, a gourd,
which, she was told, was filled with snake vertebrae covered with a loose web of beads and vertebrae, who cried
"It is I, lamerci, papa", while ringing a small bell. She
never saw her again. Her mother Ursule Bridgette, as
première reine, the first queen in the d'état-majeur, and
Tanti Cyrillia as deuxième reine, the second queen. She
would remember everything.

He was buried on the compound with African cer-
emonials after the Roman Catholic priests had performed a sacred mass for this good soul. The Congo
people sang their own strange sacred litanies over the
grave as the sun went down, the twilight lingering, the
town still, the echo of the drums for Ghede Nimbo reverberating, loud, in the Laventille hills, they seemed
to be calling "the old people" to take their "sonny-boy
home."

5. LA SIRÈNE ROSA

Ursule Bridgette dutifully performed the all the necessary rites and rituals for the retrieving of Ti-Pap's Gros Bon Ange from the souls of the dead who lived in the waters under the Earth. She took the paquet congo, the small package, wound around many times with twine, which served as his magical protection against illness and evil spirits, from his cottage, and looked at it ruefully: it had not worked for him, she thought as she placed it in her grandmother's beautiful old Govi, together with Ti-Pap's gift to her of the little carved mermaid, with long wavy hair, a sensuous tail and somewhat staring eyes, its hands held up, palms turned towards the little mouth, that seemed to be saying "Ooohhaa", and the gold coin that had been given to her by her Mohammedan patient which was struck with the image of an elephant.

"Ah, Cyrillia, this is a blow to us, I feel it in my heart, Ti-Pap, Ti-Pap, how I will miss you, Godfather, friend and brother." The tears flowed in large drops down her face, a face now grown gaunt, her eyes sunken, hollow and dark-rimmed. Her hands, now like bony yellow claws, the veins lifted from the thin skin, trembled as she tore away at the dry palm leaves, shredding them for the ceremony of chirer ayizan for protection and purification that she would hold under the patronage Ayizan and Loco, the holy parents.

"We have to do for that old werewolf, Ursule, we must send him back to hell, which parts he come out from. Why he do that, eh? That old man never do he nothing."

"He do that to break me, Cyrillia, he do that to destroy all this." She raised her hands and eyes to take in the high ceilinged sunlit upstairs drawing room at George Street, which contained the fine French furniture of the Ancien Régime acquired by her Papa, where was hung the almost life-sized oil painting, framed in gold-leaf, of his Mama, her grandmother, the Countess de Molé.

"You know, Ti-Pap did tell me, long ago, Papa had just died, that that evil man, that creature, had come with us from Saint-Domingue in a box. He had something for Mama Freda, Ti-Pap say he use to watch her, he was small, nobody didn't know where he come from, he envied her, her beauty, jealous of the way the Loa recognised her, how the old Grand Erzulie, the one before Mama, who came with two canes, she could not walk again, to see Mama dance in her peristyle. Perhaps he wanted to be like her, to be a woman, a Goddess of Love, I don't know, Cyrillia."

Just then Louis Rémy arrived with La Sirène Rosa. "What you making, Mama, what is that?"

"This is for the dance tonight, Tanti Cyrillia is helping me to make the decorations, come and give her a kiss." The little girl skipped over and put the little finger of her right hand out, Cyrillia took it and smiled "Ba mwen on ti bo, chéwi," and leaned forward to be kissed. "There, on ti bo, no more kisses today," she said, they all laughed.

"What is this shaking hands with only the little finger," asked Louis, "where has that come from?"

"It's from somewhere natural, not from me," said Ursule Bridgette.

"It's a sign, Louis," said Cyrillia, "a sign that the little one has inherited some gifts and retains the character of her grandma. Not so? Ursule, don't you think?"

"Perhaps, I have noticed some things, and how she speaks."

"You mean with that little hiss that she affects at times?" he asked.

"Yessss."

"You have it too, Ursule," he said.

"No, itss jussst a pretenccce, Louis, give me a little of that Crème de cassis, just a little, to pick me up."

"Listen Papa, listen to the sea." La Sirène Rosa held to his ear a sea shell, brought back from a recent excursion to Macqueripe. "Listen Papa, hear the waves."

"Oh yes my darling, I can hear the waves, take care you get splashed, ohh, look a big one coming." Sweeping her up in his arms they went rolling across the carpet. "Let's swim Papa, let's play I am a mermaid and I am saving you, wooshsss."

Cyrillia looked at Ursule Bridgette and smiled and said, "Cats don't make dogs, darling."

"Come you two, stop, now, too much wildness, Louis, she will not fall asleep and we have to go soon . . ."

"I will take her up-stairs, come my petite La Sirène. I will sing you a 'siren song'." Upstairs a petit boudoir had been made for her, already she loved white roses, lilac-scented talcum powder, 4711 Eau de Cologne, soft silk hankies, sea island cotton dresses, with broderie Anglaise and lots of lace.

> "Ange-gardien,
>
> Veillez sur moi;
>
> Ayez pitié de ma faiblesse;
>
> Couchez-vous sur mon petit lit;
>
> Suivez-moi sans cesse" . . .

◆ ◆ ◆

"Everybody coming tonight boy, tell Elvira to cook, cook plenty pelau, get a quenk, Narcisse Maze like he snake, tell she. Go quick in the market and see if you see Médor, tell him I send you for monkey brains and see if you could get a matte, big, an some iguana eggs and Congo pepper, dem boys like lizard toooo bad. When you coming back, pass in the shop by Cecil, tell him twelve bottles of rum, tell him no kakapoul rum, if he play the ass he dead, tell him I say, eh, go quick and come back, you have to fix up the place, go vit, vit, gason, alé vit!"

"I want the big bag."

"Bag, bag, use your hat your head so damn big."

The old man was excited, charged up with his victory against the people whom he perceived as his worst enemies.

"He dead, he dead, he dead, the old ass, dead, who he think he is, eh?" He was dragging himself along with his hands, sitting on a box-cart with four pram wheels that he had built for himself; his legs, wrecked by arthritis, could no longer bear him.

The track that led from his abode in the old La Fantaisie estate slave barracks to the estate cemetery, which was dominated by the ruined Gothic tomb of the Baron de Mallevault, was lit by the dappled sunlight of the early Corpus Christi morning.

"The boy turning out, eh, he give it to Ti-Pap good. All ah dem praying, saying chaplet, praying, to dis Orisha dat Saint. Is me who is Maît', master, me, dey say I am malfacteur, the evildoer, the man with the powder, well dem 'fraid powder! De boy he eh 'fraid, he could manjé moun, eat people, kill dem dead."

The boy, Naza, had indeed passed his first initiation into the society, Les Cochons Sans Poils; the pigs without hair. Tonight he would be a witness to another ritual of the Society, the waking of the Zombi savane, one who had been buried in the earth, having been made a zombi, is to be awakened, to be dispatched for a purpose.

The bonfire blazed up high, illuminating the huge samaans that crowded round the old slave cemetery, throwing about the grotesque shadows of the men who sat around it. Inside the tomb the boy had followed all the instructions given to him by his Maît'; he had licked and kissed the old man's scaly crippled foot, his decrepit toes with their long black curling toenails in gratitude, with tears streaming down his face, washing those ancient feet.

He had hauled the coffin that contained the night's main attraction into the middle of the crypt in the bowels of the tomb, there was just room for four or five of them and for him. He would perch in the now empty alcove that had previously contained a marble statue of Saint Ignacio López de Loyola to whom the Baron had been devoted.

Outside the men feasted, drank and celebrated the death of old Ti-Pap and the entering into their midsts of a new Cochon.

"Fresh pork, eh Narcisse, the boy good too bad!" shouted the old man; "léfan té ka valé kalbas, pas li konnèt bonda-li." Which for the benefit of the ignorant means: the elephant can swallow a calabash because it knows the size of its asshole.

"You train him, Zinga, you train him. But leh we go, we have work to do tonight, not so?"

"Take care he bite you, eh, he is bite."

"Yes, yes, these Cochons getting dronk on Cecil Marquis rum, they belly full a snake and lizard. Leh we go, leh we go."

"Help Zinga there, Zilet, before he break he neck in the tomb."

Stumbling down the steep stair, they squeezed in as best they could; those who could not fit, and those who preferred the rum and what was left of the quenk and the macajuel stew, the iguana eggs and Congo peppers, were glad to stay outside.

They had seen the corps cadavre come out of the box, bazodee with fright, he thought he was dead, he think this is hell, they all had stories of zombis who had dropped dead for true in fright, others who got out, got away and bolted into some white people garden party, his shroud buss up, all he big long toto outside. "You was there for that eh? You remember the night Muzumbo dead, they had the wake in San Fernando, you could remember, eh, eh?"

The noise and excited talk was hardly audible down inside the crypt. In fact there was no excitement at all. The flambeau illuminated the scene that was dominated by the large white coffin around which the old man, Narcisse, Phillibert, Zilet and another called Ozie were closest. "This Shampwel, this society is called to order and come tonight to do the work of le Baron Samedi, lord and guardian of this graveyard," intoned Narcisse, pouring rum on the coffin and on the ground all around. Ozie was beating a syncopated rhythm on a small drum. The old man raised himself up, there was no pain in his twisted legs, his frame, big, strong still, threw a massive shadow on the wall, partly covering the alcove in which the boy, Naza, crouched.

"Here, put this on, tie it on your face, le cadavre full of datura and dead crapaud powder." He passed the red satin squares around, then struck a match into an old chamber pot which immediately blazed with several small explosions, filling the crypt with black smoke. "Now take this." He passed around a rum bottle filled with a thick oily substance that smelled of asafoetida and tar. "Rub it, rub it, on you arm, now take the fire." With that he plunged his hands into the flaming pot and passed the fire from his hands to the hands held out by the others. For a brief moment they all appeared to be ablaze as the leaping flames caught their shirts and beards. In a frenzy they slapped each other to out the fire, laughing hysterically, screaming, shouting "Vini, Samedi, vini, vini gadé, ou, serviteur!" The little drum beating, beating louder and louder.

At a point considered appropriate, the old man with the aid of Phillibert prized open the coffin to size the corps cadavre by the shoulders, to rise him up into the night, to bring him to the prison of his new condition. For a brief second, the old man did see the staring eyes open in the coal-black face of the man who was once known as Saint Jacques. The next second, the body sat up straight, and grabbed him by the throat like a vice.

Men screamed, Narcisse and Phillibert tried to prize open the hand, the po capsized, sending the flaming liquid to the ground, towards them, those who could make the stairs, scrambled up, others aflame, tried to, the coffin fell over, taking the old man and his killer to ground, where they fought like beast. The coffin, now on fire with the flammable liquid, burned upon them where they were. Then, they lay still, quiet, they were both dead.

The boy, Naza, had seen it all. Singed like a chicken, his hair, eyebrows and clothes burnt and in rags, he scrambled down from his perch and out of the tomb. The others had fled, howling, laughing, into the pitch-black, wooded hillside above La Fantaisie Road. What a story.

The gruesome deaths at Rue La Fantaisie in Sainte-Anne did not make the papers. It was, however, the talk of the Town.

"My God, Cyrillia, what a thing! The old loup garou is dead at last, praise the Bondyé, good riddance, good riddance. But it is Saint Jacques, they take him, eh?"

"It look so, I miss him, he come every Saturday for his little money, but he eh come since week before last, and with Ti-Pap's death and everything, I forget him."

"Oh Cyrillia, you understand what really went on there, you realise that they kill Ti-Pap and take Saint Jacques to turn him into a zombi, that old, old man, they do that to hurt me, you, Louis, the child, this place, the work."

"These people are hell, poor Saint Jacques, he was a good soul, Sisi, Maze daughter, tell me that they find the two of them, the old Bokor and Saint Jacques in the bottom of the vault burn up, Saint Jacques, hand on the Bokor throat, the fingers inside the flesh, where he hold him in the wind pipe, like he want to rip it out, you ever hear more, Ursule, you ever?"

"Cyrillia, these people is work for the devil, you know, they take him and put him in the grave, then dig him up, but you know, Saint Jacques, heself was a serviteur à deux mains, eh you know that?"

"He! I never knew that," she said, puffing on her clay pipe that had gone out.

"Yes, he served, as they say, with both his hands, us in the Rada with the right, and Obeah with the left, so he was with them too, Cyrillia, them too."

"Ah Bondyé, save me yes, you will have Retirer d'en bas de l'eau for him?"

"Of course, we will reclaim his soul from the waters of the abyss, same as Ti-Pap, darling, he came here with us, he was close to Papa, we must do this for him, for his children and grandchildren, he have family, plenty."

The events of Ti-Pap's death and those others that took place brought about a truce, in a sense, between the two confronting forces of the Town. Ursule Bridgette with the help of Cyrillia continued to serve the community in much the same way that they had always done; perhaps with less gaiety. They both became more religious in the Christian sense and were seen at the Cathedral of the Immaculate Conception on the feast days, albeit these feast days happened to coincide with the festival days of the Orisha whom they served. Ursule Bridgette developed a particular devotion to the Blessed Virgin Mary as expressed by Our Lady of Sorrows, Mater Dolorosa, names by which the Blessed Virgin Mary is referred to in relation to sorrows in her life.

Because of Ursule Bridgette's identification with her mother Erzulie Freda, she felt in her heart a strong identification with Mary, not so much as the mother of life and of God; but more as the mother of man's legend, his story of life, its significance. In a very real manner, "The Blessed Virgin Mary" and "Erzulie Freda," as Goddesses of Love to her were the very essence by which mankind conceives divinity. And as such, to man she is his mother, his lover and his fate.

From a Signor Simon Antonmattei, a Corsican merchant newly arrived in the Town, Ursule Bridgette acquired what she felt was an appropriate setting for her ancient treasure and placed the old clay Govi in a wondrously-made porcelain jar, decorated with a depiction of the Blessed Virgin Mary, accompanied by angels whom she identified as the Archangels Saint Michael and Saint Raphael.

Ursule Bridgette and Louis Rémy remained as one. His wife Marie Louise Antoinette Céleste knew of their plaçage, their 'mariage de la main gauche', and although his 'left hand marriage' grieved her heart and served to destroy her respect for him, it did not take away the love that she felt. Louis was a boring person, but was good, kind and at least consistent, she told herself. How did she deal with him when he came home from his mulatresse and wanted to have her, then and there, well that was their business. What we know is that she did not have any more children for him after the birth of their last daughter, and that was fourteen or fifteen years before he died.

6. Amélie Eugénie:-

KI MÉLÉ WÒZ NAN PAKÉ BWA JACQUES?
What business has a rose in Jacques' bundle of wood?

Amélie Eugénie Maximilien, my grandmother, was a boarder at Saint Joseph's Convent when she saw for the first time the person by whom her entire life would be shaped. Never getting the whole story straight myself, I can only relate this by the haphazard assemblage of inferences, dropped hints, loose talk, innuendo, and of course, my own imagination.

She had attended the wedding of Juanita de Medina, a person she hardly knew, because of the insistence of her mother. The wedding party over, she sat in the gathering dark in a pool of boredom at the top of the marble front steps of the now quiet house; a rising heat foretold rain. Her parents and those of Juanita de Medina and some others were enjoying one of those indeterminable goodbye's that baffle teenagers, when she saw coming towards her through the darkened lower storey, lit by the intermittent flashes of the lightning of the gathering storm, a tall girl, who became illuminated for a brief second.

There was a sense of suspended stillness, of time passing slowly. For some reason she felt compelled to rise and enter the drawing room. The debris of the wedding celebration lay about. Flowers, weary of their arrangement, furniture still placed for, but now deprived of conversation, wine bottles, empty of their potential, the cake, alone, devoid of complements, glasses drained, bouquets thrown, confetti relieved of gaiety lay about the floor, a dotty Carnivalesque pattern that led to the bottom of a flight of stairs leading to the bedrooms on the upper floor. She took them quickly and entered a light that came from an open doorway at the far end of the corridor.

The girl was standing at a window. Outside a powerful wind buffeted the house in gusts that came every few seconds, producing a noise not dissimilar to howling. Between these blasts, the sound of the rain was like the hammering of thousands of huge, elongated molten drops that drove themselves into the wooden shingles of the roof with force. Lifting some, while sending others spinning away into the darkness, the enormous drops, driven by a powerful velocity, dislocated garden tiles, smashed through leaves, and emptied the dirt out of plant pots. Suddenly it was still, except for the roar of the guttering, and the sound of the rain striking the window panes.

She stood at the girl's side; the onrush of the storm and the attraction to the strange girl frightened her a little.

The wind, upon returning, empowered the downpour, to wash the gallery furniture off into the garden and into the mud of the devastated flower beds. They looked as multiple flashes of lightning illuminated the bending and twisting of the huge forest trees into hideous, alarming caricatures of themselves. A resounding clap of thunder that was simultaneous with a phantasmal flash made both of them jump out of their skins and in to each other's arms.

"La Parole était au commencement; la Parole était avec Dieu, et cette Parole était Dieu," prayed the girl. To which my grandmother responded:

"Elle était au commencement avec Dieu."

"Bondyé, sa sé tonnè."

Another huge flash of lightning illuminated the world — and was followed instantaneously by an even louder clap of thunder.

"Toutes choses ont été faites par elle,"

And together.

"Et rien de ce qui a été fait n'a été fait sans elle.

"C'est en elle qu'était la vie et la vie était la lumière des hommes."

They had to laugh. "Lapli ka tonbé," said the girl.

"The thunder frightens me too, bad," said Amélie, my grandmother. "My name is Amélie. I wish my parents would come."

"Tonné ka fè pè mé zéklè ka tjwé, Mine is La Sirène Rosa, call me Rosa."

"Rosa, Rosa! Time to go, the rain is easing up just now, come and say good-bye. You have met Madame

Maximilien's daughter, they are looking for you too, ma chè, come girls."

Ursule Bridgette and the girls came down as the others were gathering, outside the coachmen were doing their best to keep the startled horses in hand and themselves dry.

"Au revoir!" "Au revoir!" made the rounds as everyone left in an increasing drizzle.

"Au revoir, Rosa."

"Au revoir, Amélie."

They did not see each other really for nearly a year although they were both under the care of the French nuns of the Order of the Sisters of St. Joseph of Cluny. Then one Easter Sunday morning, quite suddenly, they found themselves sitting side by side in the Convent chapel. "Are you leaving school?" she whispered.

"Yes."

"When?"

"Next week."

Holy Mass over, they joined the crowd.

"Christ is risen."

"Christ is risen!"

"Next week?"

"Yes. Christ is risen."

People were leaving, families forming into familiar formats, the wind blew hats away, ribbons fluttered, skirts flew up, everyone laughed.

"Christ is risen!"

Amélie was just past thirteen years of age when she met La Sirène Rosa for the first time. Rosa was then 15; she, Amélie, came of a well-known respected family from the pass-for-white wealthy upper-class that acquired "acceptability" amongst in the colony's whites, both the local béké and the British, because of her father—he was the island's most skilled surgeon—but also because of her mother, who had much more blue blood in her veins than all the Tan-tans put together, and more than that even: she, from time to time, entertained exotic-titled personages from abroad, who were received at Government House. Her mother also possessed much better sapphires; these, set in diamonds, obviously came with an inheritance worth envying, and then they were rich, and travelled regularly to the United States and Europe.

She, Amélie, loved La Sirène Rosa proudly, but secretly, from the start. But without defiance of her mother's sensibilities: these regarded and analyzed the subtle tones and shades of people on a daily basis, which were measured in minuté, the results dictated who was acceptable in her drawing room, and who had to pass in the back. La Sirène Rosa definitely had to pass in the back. She was too dark. Her mother was the mistress of Louis Rémy, and was as well a known sorceress. But, the question remained, how did the mother have so much money? That was a mystery, one that could only be compared to how she was able to gain entry to, and so obviously have the ear of the oldest and most respected French families of Port-d'Espagne?

6. AMÉLIE EUGÉNIE

◆ ◆ ◆

For the well-off, property-owning European society of Trinidad of the 1850s and 60s, the island offered the best of all worlds. European men of a certain age and older continued to wear a coat, waistcoat and breeches buttoned to the knee with stockings, buckled shoes, their hair in a queue, and wore, if they thought them-selves entitled, a sword. The young men, however, wore long trousers, called pantaloons, with smart cutaway jackets in a variety of shades with horn, silver, or brass buttons, cravats and soft sea island cotton shirts and leather boots imported from England, and carried a stick.

White women developed a distinctive style of dress. They always wore white, highlighted sometimes by fou-lards at their necks and handkerchiefs from the Indies on their heads, in the manner of the gracious ladies of Bordeaux. They stayed in the shade until late afternoon in preservation of their complexions and devised tiny, often hilarious beauty marks, which they hid upon their persons so as to delight their lovers. Familial incest was condoned for the procreation of additional Catholics and the maintenance of pedigree.

The land, cultivated, was dedicated to agriculture and to the rearing of live-stock. Warehouses on the Plaza de la Marina were fully stocked with goods in anticipation of rich rewards: hogsheads brimmed with sugar, rum and molasses, cocoa there was aplenty, and varieties of coffee; nutmeg, cloves and mace arrived from Grenada, tobacco and cotton from Tobago, tonka beans, peppers and cinnamon from everywhere.

Exotic fruit soaked silently in demijohns of alcohol, waiting to become after-dinner curiosities for parvenus of the café society of Paris, London or Basle. Other warehouses were filled to overflowing with all manner of champagne, brandy and wines, moiré-patterned satin, velvets, taffetas, laces, French umbrellas, truffles, cheeses, dried fruit, galvanised nails, farm machinery, gun powder, bayonets, cannon balls and all else that was required to live in style in the tropics.

Just about everybody spoke French and/or Patois. The mixed race, les gens de couleur, yearned for acceptance, for money, for education, for lighter complexions and for respect. The slowly arriving East Indians were hardly noticed. The Chinese, few, were ignored. Everybody wore hats. Black men and women carried, fetched, worked in the houses, the gardens, the yards of everybody, as all manner of servants; black tradesmen made masonry, hammered, sawed and plumbed, some picked and shovelled, whacked and chopped, others dug and hacked; while some simply abandoned themselves to idleness and did nothing but sit in the shade to drink kakapoul rum whole day.

Black and coloured women who did not come from the Protestant islands wore the gorgeous costumes of the French Antilles. Sumptuary laws there forbade them to dress in a style even remotely similar to that of white women, so they devised the picturesque à la Capresse style of dress, which consisted of a rich and valuable Madras turban, tastefully tied so as to indicate the availability or disinclination of the wearer to masculine advances, which was worn in lieu of the forbidden cap or bonnet. In place of the gown, that was also disallowed, they wore a 'jupe,' a skirt in shades to match the beautiful turban, over which there was an apron of 'linon,' which was decorated with little pockets, embroidered and fringed. Petticoats, of course, of 'linon' with much embroidery and Breton lace. A smartly plaited and fringed chemisette, with sleeves reaching but halfway to the elbow, clasped by large gold buttons; a heavy necklace and gold earnings, large, and as fragile as eggshells, and a lovely Indian kerchief with which they might cover the charms of their decolleté.

All black women served and washed, iron and starched, cared for and minded everyone, black as well as white; some were loved, others despised, while a few became the cherished and, in secret, ancestresses of "pass for white" beauties who went on to live in antebellum mansions in the State of North Carolina.

There was good music and bad. There were masked balls held in elegant townhouses where absurd liaisons produced idiotic children, conceived in alcoholic stupor. There were the religious, the pagan, the agnostic and the repugnant. There were some who lived in the splendour of total solitude in enormous wooden mansions deep in the forested interior of the island, while others loved the shady streets and steep-stepped lanes of Port-of-Spain. In the harbour road, fast clippers, commodious merchant men, elegant brigantines and royal Man-of-War of His Britannic Majesty's ocean-going battle fleets turned at anchor in the largest and most beautiful harbour in the Caribbean.

◆ ◆ ◆

"Somebody, I forget now who, said to me that Jab Molassi, the Molasses Devil, was the start of cannes brûlées. It's the worst thing that can happen on an estate: a slave meets death by falling into the vat of boiling molasses," said La Sirène Rosa. The girls were on their own in town, or so they thought. Cyrillia had sent Orphilia, Saint Jacques' granddaughter, to keep an eye on them.

Cyrillia knew that Amélie was technically supposed to be in the company of the Metiviers, a family of opticians, but also knew that she had slipped away from them, and into a band of Jou ouvè revellers dressed as cats, whose meowing call — "Jou ouvè ?" Is it day break? — was answered, "Jou pankò ouvè!" It is not yet day. This was shouted against an assortment of batteria that included bicycle frames, wooden crates, bugles, cow bells, and the striking, with an iron nail, of the antique stirrups that once belonged to old Captain d'Herrera after whom Henry was later named. The band, organised by the younger members of the Cadiz family, had appeared out of Cadiz Road in Belmont, and swept her into Town.

Having made a successful run for it, Amélie spotted
Rosa from across the top of Marine Square. She was
sitting in the little square at the back of the Cathedral
where the village of Port-d'Espagne once buried their
dead. She was waiting for her. Amélie's heart was in her
throat, pounding.

They had promised to meet on Fat Monday, and were
now standing amongst the crowd on the pavement outside Mme. Maupertuis' house, opposite to the Roman
Catholic Cathedral on the corner of George Street,
looking at the Carnival.

"Ti nèg gwo-siwo. The molasses devil is the ghost of
the sugar estate?"

"So they say. And the Jab Jab, the whip-cracking,
mirrored one, with the red and green satin skirts and
orange stockings, is the Papa of the Dragon Band, the
Devil's Band."

"How you know all that Rosa? I feel you make up all
sorts of things to frighten me, sometimes."

"Sé pou on dòmi an poulyési-poul pou sav si yo ka
ronflé. It's true, a long time ago old Monsieur Scamaroni, inspired by a sacred picture illustrating the exorcis-
ing of the Devil from a sick person, on display in a shop
at Calle de San Luis, brought out the first Devil Band,
he and a young half-Chinese boy named Jones."

"What did you say? You know I don't understand Patois so good."

"Sé pou on dòmi an poulyési-poul pou sav si yo ka
ronflé." Means, 'you must sleep with fowls to know if
they snore'."

They could hear the call of the chantwell and the answer of a chorus, and the drums getting nearer– boom! boom—boom! Reverberating in their chests, they sounded as though they were being beaten inside of a very deep well.

. . ."Ti manmay-la, bay mwen lavwa!" from the chantwell.

"Ti manmay-la, bay mwen lavwa!" answered the chorus.

"Look the Devil there, Rosa, he is terrifying, look they coming," said Amélie, pointing at the devil band that was approaching with speed down Nelson Street at the back of the Cathedral. "Let's run."

"See, how they have cow horns and rope tails," said Rosa. "Mama said when you see cow horns, that is bad business. These have flexible wings, that means they can fly like Jack Spaniard bull fighters."

The band comprised of about 70 or 80 men and women, carrying long forks and dressed in black and red. Everyone wore small face masks. There were presidents and princes with elaborate costumes, covered with brass buttons and gold fringe, diamanté spangles and gold cord. There was one central character called Lucifer who wore a golden crown and was even more elaborately costumed. He was portrayed by Gilbert Scamaroni himself and used a large head mask imported from Germany by the firm Waterman Brothers of Frederick Street.

"Look Amélie, Beelzebub, Lord of the Flies, these others, they must be the flies around him, look, bum bum flies, horse flies, gad flies. A trouser fly?"

"Oh Rosa, I will have to go to confession, too much Devil business, look how he is in an iron cage and bound by nine chains."

The Beelzebub was made of papier mâché, fearsome in character, the entire contraption was carried aloft on poles.

"There have Satan too."

"Tanti Cyrillia say the Beast coming out for the first time this year, a man they call 'Georgie' playing that. She says the Beast costume is made of large fish scales and so constructed that they could bustle up or be made to lie flat."

Satan came up to them. A tall man, elegant, in a top hat, his face fiercely made up, his black satin cape lined in red velvet, was real. He was dressed in the uniform of a grand duke, with scarlet sashes and jewelled orders, and carried a ceremonial sword in his hand; a boy dressed as a page carried his book and long feathery quill, ready to record their sins.

"Joyeux lundi gras. May I kiss your hands, Mamzèl?" he asked with an elegant, courtly bow.

"Noo!" they screamed, leaping up, and bolted through the Square to the grass market on the other side.

Before Satan came and startled them Amélie's attention had been caught by a horned figure who was mincing and cringing up to them like a beggar; then Satan was standing before them with his court of sycophants hovering. The figure disappeared; later they watched a mimed play that none but the pantomimists themselves could comprehend. A man disguised as a coffin and carrying a skeleton stalked by. Another costumed as a cello played itself. A live black cat looked out from the Queen of Heart's hairpiece.

"They have real dwarves, Amé, look, they are old men, some dragging chains to which are attached souls waiting to be reincarnated from slavery, look the souls are old shoe soles."

"Who was that, Rosa, just now?"

"That was Monsieur Drago, the Italian man with the cocoa store, you see how everything he wearing real, no costume, the real thing. He is with the Franc Maçons, Amélie, they have white people here who is deal, real science men. You ever see those Drago children? They real weird oui?"

Amélie hadn't meant Satan, she was referring to the horned creature dressed in dry banana leaves. He scared her.

"Come, let's go to your house; now, it's too hot and I can't see any more Devils today, I can't stay long, the Metiviers must be looking for me by now, but I have to wee-wee."

◆ ◆ ◆

They were both now in their late teens, and were in-
separable, in spite of objections from Amélie's parents.
This was vexatious for Amélie. Even more vexatious was
Rosa's beau, a man who was expected later, after she
had gone. He was a regular visitor of their household, it
would appear, but somehow invisible. Amélie had never
met Rosa's beau, although Rosa had spoken of him in
an off-hand manner, as though Amélie should know everything about him already. Amélie did not know anyone with a beau, Hortense de Bouillon had a fiancé and
Clémence Rochard was hoping to get one soon, and
Victorine Farquhar had one, but not any longer, and
that was why she was in Barbados having a baby, which
is a secret and must not be mentioned.

Amélie felt uncomfortable whenever she thought of
Rosa with "her beau," utterly left out, not included in
something obviously their own. She had no beau, she
had no one, friends or anything like that. She had no
cousins either, just her brothers and sisters: her Mama
was from France and her Papa was an only child. Rosa
was her friend, her only friend.

That night she went up to bed early. The exertions
of the day, the heat, the noise of the Carnival, had giv-
en her a headache, and she also wanted to avoid what
would no doubt be an unpleasant conversation with
her mother. She wanted the oblivion of sleep. It was
as though, suddenly, there was so much to think about,
Rosa's beau, her mother's insistence that she leave "her
childish ways" behind and end this friendship with what
her mother described as "an unsuitable individual", and

now this persistent but vague disquiet. She stood at her open bedroom window, it was a hot night.

"You can go now, Fifine," she said without turning.

"Thank you, Miss Amé, I put some warm water in the basin for you, and there is a towel in a bowl with cool water for your headache. I hope you feel better. . ."

"Thank you, Fifine, I hope so too."

"Turn off the lamp, Miss Amé?"

"No thank you, I will read for a while."

She settled into the soft wide bed, the cool cloth across her forehead was a comfort and the soft glow of her lamp caused a sense of ease, the feeling that something weighty was falling away from her. She picked up a little book, it was a Litany of the Saints, opened it at random and read:

"O God, come to my assistance; O Lord, make haste to help me.

"Let them be confounded and ashamed that seek my soul. Let them be turned backward and blush for shame, that desire evils to me.

"Let them be presently turned away blushing for shame that say to me: 'Tis well, 'Tis well.

"Let all that seek Thee rejoice and be glad of Thee. Let such as love Thy salvation say always: The Lord be magnified."

She closed the little book, reached over and turned the flame in the lamp out. The room seemed cooler, a gentle wind lifted the window's lace curtain and blew softly across her face and she fell gratefully to sleep.

She became gradually awake, it seemed like coming up to the surface, the dream, no longer remembered, fading, leaving a taste so bitter in her mouth and 'a smell, aloes', she said to herself, her mouth was so dry, she felt nauseous and tried to turn but couldn't. She opened her eyes and screamed with all her might into the black face of the thing that was squatting, sort of sitting across her. It snorted. She screamed again. The figure squealed, and, grunting like a pig, leaped from the bed and bounded to and through the window and across the lawn squealing and honking. A smell, like tata. The door opened her father, her mother, Fifine. Lights, darkness.

" . . . . . ?"

'Tis well, 'Tis well, said a voice in her head, and chuckled.

"It was a bad dream, ma chérie, everything is alright, Papa is outside with his gun and Victor, come, drink some water, oh you have a little fever, come I think you've had an accident, come and sit on the posy, I will get something to wipe you."

There was no need for her to use the chamberpot in its chair in the corner of the room, and she did not need to be wiped, she had not had an accident.

"What was that smell?" Her mother stood at the window looking out into the darkness of the garden, a warm wind was picking up, it carried the smell of the mangrove forest East of the town, and promised rain. She couldn't stop crying, there was a man, she told them, he was there, here. Look. But there was no mark, no stain, and the yard was empty.

"The dogs did not bark, and you know them, they bark at the wind, no it was a dream, you know you have dreams, you have not had one for a long time, come drink this, Fifine made this for you, lime bud tea, she said, drink, Fifine will stay with you, come, into bed, it's a quarter to three."

Her earliest memories spoke to her of a secret understanding of what next, how come? And if this, that, or the other had happened or was about to happen. Sometimes she would know just before, especially if she had dreamed. She was always a little distracted by the anticipation of events that had not taken place, but possessed the potentiality of becoming. Small things anticipated, then actualised. She was then a little thing herself, and moved in a world of small consequences.

At times, she would fall into a shallow sleep and see, in truth feel, the emotions, as a course of events unfolded that may have taken place day before yesterday, to which she had not been a witness.

At other times, she would have a clear understanding of what was forthcoming, like for instance when, just fourteen or fifteen, she came home from the wedding of Juanita de Medina and told her father that he should remove all his important papers from his office because a fire is going to burn down the Chronicle building next door to his office on Frederick Street, and the old mansion that housed his medical practice will go up in flames because of a lack of water in the City's fire brigade appliance. Knowing his daughter's odd, at times uncanny, abilities, Dr. Maximilien did remove some of his moveable and more expensive surgical equipment and some of his case material from his office.

The next morning he was awakened by his yardman, Victor, shouting outside his bedroom window, to inform him that there was a big fire in town.

It was this faculty, this insight into the order of things, that brought herself and Rosa Rémy together in the first place. She knew that Rosa was a part of her life's scheme of things, which she perceived like a chessboard, wide and far reaching, stretching before and behind her, rising, falling, curving and flattening out, leading to a wide variety of destinations, both viable and hopeless as possibilities.

If she followed the white squares, she could go in this direction, if the black, then another. With great difficulty she could change course and move to the other course of events. Rosa was in both the white and the black. Her future was bound up with hers. She wondered if they had shared one or more past existences. She told Rosa all this, explaining it, to her surprise, better than she had understood it herself; to her great relief and satisfaction Rosa understood perfectly.

During a walk in the Royal Botanic Gardens in Port-of-Spain one hot afternoon in May, when she was about seventeen and Rosa two or three years older, she had the clear presentiment that they would kiss and they did. It was a simple kiss, but it held the potentiality of a future which contained both happiness and grief. She knew that. What she did not know was that they were being observed by an ugly man hidden in the branches of a nutmeg tree.

The checkerboard stretched out before her and she could see a long life together, happy sunny memories, then trouble, but solvable, dark horror, fear, parting.

Two weeks after Carnival, she went to the George Street house and told Rosa of her experiences on the evening of lundi gras. It had taken her a few days to catch herself. An incipient fever lingered and turned into a cough that kept her awake, listening to the night. She found La Sirène Rosa distracted by her mother's sudden illness, at her wit's end, attempting to deal with the fear and with the anticipation of the worst that could happen.

"Oh ma chérie, that is so frightening Amé, that was no dream, you know that, that man is bad he is a Bokor, an evil spirit that takes the form of an animal, a daemon, that is what he send for you."

"No, no Rosa, that was no daemon, that was a man. You know I saw that man, in the morning when we were looking at the Devil Band, I saw him coming towards us, just when Monsieur Drago came up, remember?"

"Yes, you were upset that day, but Amé, we will talk about that later, I am so worried about Mamy I want you to dream for me, I want to know what is going to happen, please, come let's go in the gallery, I will push in the drawing room doors."

The Cathedral bells tolled for the Angelus, it was mid-day. Amélie lay back in the old rocking chair in the gallery overlooking the quiet street and fell into a shallow sleep, rocking very slowly, her head turned to one side. Rosa sat by her side on a small wooden bench. "What you seeing Amé?" asked Rosa in a small voice.

"Can you see Mamy, is she getting better?"

"No, Rosa," was the answer.

"Amé?"

"Yes."

"Is Mamy going to die?"

"Yes."

"When?"

"Now."

And so it was. Ursule Bridgette passed away in the heat of the day that very afternoon.

There was consternation and grief. Mourning, lamentation and profound sorrow that went on for months. At first Amélie was removed from it. But because it affected Rosa profoundly and because of her love for Rosa she was absorbed into the grief, and shared in the anguish and felt the loss, the heartbreak and the despair caused by it all.

Ursule Bridgette had suffered a stroke that paralysed the left side of her body and left her speechless. Her condition deteriorated during the course of the morning, and by mid-afternoon what Amé had seen in her dream occurred. There was no opportunity to discuss the circumstances that had brought such evil into her bed.

Cyrillia took charge of the household and dealt with all the arrangements with regard to the funeral services. The first was held at the Roman Catholic Cathedral of the Immaculate Conception, and the other in the mountain grotto where Ursule Bridgette had communicated with the Goddesses. And then there was the funeral, an enormous affair at the Lapéyrouse cemetery.

Criers were dispatched to the four quarters of the island to inform communities, Orisha societies, individuals, the living and the dead. People came from Moruga, Lengua, Siparia, Bourg Mulatresse, Brasso Benoît and Brasso Seco, Toco, Tacarigua, Tunapuna, Chacachacare and Carapichaima. The train station bustled with mourners who arrived dressed in what occurred to them to be the appropriate national costume suitable for such an auspicious occasion. They came with food, flags, drums, effigies of the saints, reliquaries containing the teeth, knuckle joints, ankle bones and the oracular jaw bones of the truly obscure who had passed from this world on other islands during strikes, rebellions, uprisings, wars of liberation that had been lost as the result of the superior fire power of European troops.

They came. They filled the house, camped in the garden, sought, and were given accommodation in the houses of neighbours, with members of the household's extended family and with total strangers. There were at any time, over a period of several month, various forms of services, rituals and feasts being held in the backyard where the one hundred year-old morocoys stalked indifferent to the hullabaloo, the drumming, chanting, bell-ringing, candle-burning and mourning for the death of a person so well-beloved that she would be spoken of in the present tense for generations after her demise.

Cyrillia was the tower of strength, the rock of ages who knew what to do, who to talk to, how to arrange, disarrange and discontinue. Which is what she did after an unpleasant incident which involved two opposing Shango societies having it out in front of the Angostura Bitters factory that had taken over the premises once occupied by the Catholic Cathedral's Presbytery.

The inevitable moment of choice came. La Sirène Rosa knew that it was to be Cyrillia, who, now as première reine, the first queen in the d'état-majeur, would take charge of the work, the Retirer d'en bas de l'eau; the elaborate rituals, ceremonies, feasts and sacrifices appropriate for the reclaiming of the Gros Bon Ange of Ursule Bridgette from the waters of the abyss. It would not be her.

These awesome tasks completed, what followed was a dance de réjouissance, a thanksgiving and a reception for the new Queen. La Sirène Rosa looked in admiration, her eyes brimming, at this tall stately, serenely beautiful woman. Her face, the face of her people, now at a great age, dressed in all the colourful regalia of the Grand Erzulie Freda, attended by her lovely young serviteurs in long white dresses and white turbans, receiving her guest by proffering the little finger of her right hand, dancing gracefully as the big maman drum played the bélè for La Reine Rivé, the chorus singing "She, who is the most admired, auspiciously beloved, most often bound in the sacred matrimony of the devoted and the divine has come, the Goddess of Love, the Queen arrives!" Dancing round with slow and fluid movements to the heavy vibration of the drums, her patterned skirts lifted to display her embroidered and lace-trimmed petticoats, her strong arched dancer's feet, she smiled into the eyes of the child that she still saw in Rosa. As the cadence of the drums quickened, moved by the poignancy of the moment, caught up in the part, la Reine Cyrillia wept and cried out that she is not loved enough.

With tenderness and with gentle caresses all the young serviteurs comforted her, and fanned her, the handsome young sailor who had been holding one of the four chandelles in the peristyle came swiftly forward for her to put her ancient foot into his lap as she sat enthroned. Orphilia danced towards her and placed a lovely silken kerchief around her shoulders, and La Sirène Rosa presented her with French perfume and rose scented talcum, and offered her a collier of fine red-gold beads and a little crystal glass of Crême de Menthe. Others came to pay homage, to offer libations, give gifts and throw the petals of roses that were cultivated only for this purpose, on the ground where she walked. No one present that beautiful night would ever forget how the bélè drums rolled, the dancers twirled, the Loa came, and the old Gods, laughing, took possession of their faithful horses.

◆ ◆ ◆

"So that's him, he is so old."

They were lying in Rosa's bed, looking at photographs that they had laid out on the bed as though they were Tarot cards, while enjoying Crème de Menthe, with ice! Ice was the colony's newest novelty. In fact, they were alone, as everyone in the house had gone to join the crowds, who were thronging the Saint Vincent Street jetty so as to see ice, or just experience the sensation of the cool draft of air as the ice wagons, drawn by enormous white mules, went by.

"He is not old, Amé, he is mature, and is very nice, and sweet. I have known him now for almost twenty years."

"Do you lie with him, Rosa?" asked Amélie. She had not "lain" with anyone, although she had been kissed once by André Bollard at a dance given at the Metiviers, and a few times by Rosa.

"Yes, of course darling, we have made love, right here in this bed from the time I was sixteen, he is my man, my lover, me darlin'."

"Oh Rosa, how could you? It's a sin, it's adultery, he has a wife and ten children, he is old enough to be your father, he is a friend of my father, for heaven's sake!"

"Five children," said La Sirène Rosa.

"Look, Amé, this is our world, it's very different from yours, although you sprang from the same beginnings as this."

"What you mean?"

"Oh Amé, your Papa is Monsieur de Montalembert's son with Eugénie Roussillac, your grandmother. What was she? She was a black."

"She was not black, Rosa."

"She was une femme de couleur, a coloured woman, Amé, fair-skinned, but did not behave or even look like a white woman, if she had a sister, the sister could have come out looking like me. Mixed-up people like us are like that. Look at your brother Jean-Paul, he is brown-skinned, darker than any of you by far, your sister Clarisse, she is fair but has bad hair. And look at you. You look white, you act like a white person sometimes, you look more than white, you have red hair, red freckles and blue blue eyes, but you have a beautiful backside that no white woman could possibly hope to possess. You are a very beautiful sang-mêlée, my own belle-bois, do not think about Claude," she kissed her softly on the mouth. "Petits amoureux aux plumes." Little feathered loves, they called their kisses.

"Claude is a part of my life, a very important part. We do not live in plaçage as Mama and Papa did, but he comes to me, and I go to him, we are intimate, he helps me with the estate. I cannot live like Mama did, do all that she did, the Ti Guinée, the African way, serving the Loa, the Orisha work, the feasts, the charity, the people, all of that, it's not for me. We went to the Convent. That's the thing, Amé. Cyrillia is old now, she cannot continue the compound. The others like Orphilia, and the others they do not know, and they did not come from us, our blood, Gran Ma's blood, Erzulie Freda's blood from Saint-Domingue. Claude is going to help me to leave all this."

"Oh Rosa, do you love him?"

"Of course I love him, I love him very much."

"And me?"

"I love you too, nou ké bien amizé nou, ti kakakoden-mwen."

"Yes we have fun, but Rosa don't call me kakakoden, I am not 'turkey fart in your face'. I thought you liked my freckles." They had to laugh, but Amélie was on the verge of tears. "I love you so much it hurts me in myself, I don't want you with him. I want you with me."

"I am with you, and will always be, 'ti-fanm-la dou, li dou, li dou'," she sang softly in her ear, and took her in her arms and made love to her for the first time.

My grandmother and La Sirène Rosa became "mas-sissi", lovers, their relationship, however, went some-where deeper, conveying a sense of belonging to, and longing for each other. Over time they became like twins, or how twins are imagined to be like, at times in-tuitively knowing, and becoming in a manner of speak-ing, like one person.

For as La Sirène Rosa sought to alter her life, and eventually succeeded in leaving her mother's world with the help of Claude-Ambrose du Vivier de Noailles, so too did Amélie, my grandmother, succeed in rear-ranging her own. She left her parents' house, and with money given to her by her father, she had an income and was able to set up a modest home. He understood her to some extent, and appreciated to a degree both aspects of her very original personality, the one that dreamed into the space-time continuum, a femme-dormeuse, who knew instinctively that space and duration are one and the same; and the other one, the one who loved and was loved by the sorceress's daughter.

La Sirène Rosa did leave "all this" after the death of Tanti Cyrillia. She closed the compound. The area where it had once stood became known as Stanislas Place, remembered by the people for a person who was considered by them to be a hero of the Fédon uprising in Grenada, which had taken place at the end of the previous century. It became bounded by Lovell Place, St. John Street and Laventille Road; but the children of the old members of the compound, whom she allowed to stay on the land, some of them were in fact the grand-children of the original slaves brought by the Count de Molé out of Saint-Domingue in the 1780s to Trinidad, never left the area, and maintained their commitment to the Orisha religion there for generations.

On one of La Sirène Rosa's last meetings with Tanti Cyrillia in her quarters, upstairs at the back of the George Street house, La Sirène Rosa was handed the beautiful jar that contained the old clay Govi by the now quite ancient Queen, whose wrinkled, jet black face and sharp clear eyes expressed as ever just love and concern.

"Ah Rosa, mwen ka alé, ma chè, Monsieur le Baron Samedi waits for me in the drawing room, it's time to return home to Ti Guinée, to Africa, I stayed too long, I think, what you think child, you think I know the way, eh?"

"You know the way, Tanti, do not worry."

"Ah Rosa, you know I have this keeping for you, it is time for you to take it, keep it good, it have everybody living in it, you Mama, your Papa, you Gran Mammy, even Ti-Pap there, I want you to put me there too, eh, you could bury my old bones in Lapéyrouse, but put this in there for me, and you and Orphilia know what to do, don't let me stay too long in the water under the Earth, I don't like too much water, so speak to the les Invisibles for my Gros Bon Ange for me. Hold a Danse de réjouissance for me, invite everybody, you hear."

La Sirène Rosa took her Paquet Congo from her, it was just a very small brown cloth package tied up many times over with hemp twine. So little after so long a life.

"Yes Tanti, I will put it."

If one could peer into this jar, this precious vessel, this pot-de-tête, this receptacle for the 'head', soul or mind, this Govi that contained the spirits of the dead, or the Loa, that was always left in the care of the 'gan,' the chief, of the 'houn', the spirits, the 'houngan' in the language of the Fon people of Benin, or, at times placed into the hands of the most trusted and worthy person in the family, and see inside the ragged bundles. The quaint, but in essence ordinary collection of things, could surprise, and perhaps even entertain the curious for a brief moment.

Most of the fetishes contained in the Govi were of the de Molé family. Amongst these were a black stone a little smaller than the palm of your hand, which Erzulie Freda, La Sirène Rosa's grandmother, had found on the plantation to which she had been chained on the island of Saint-Domingue, where a bolt of lightning had struck, its imagined ancient warmth still possessing the memory of the clap of thunder that had shattered the morning silence. The tattered rotting remnants of Erzulie Freda's jupé slave blouse in which a cowrie shell and red bead necklace that had belonged to her mother were wrapped, this necklace had come with her from Africa. A little plaited lock of Erzulie Freda's hair, tied with a leather thong, a collection of her toe nail clippings and two of her teeth. From Peletan de Molé there was a gold ring with a red stone upon which was engraved his family's coat of arms.

From La Sirène Rosa's mother, Ursule Bridgette, there was a piece of lace from the dress that she had worn one miraculous night, a long narrow red velvet ribbon that tied a lock of thick black hair, and a golden Guinée that bore on its obverse an elephant. A tiny mermaid, carved from ebony with long wavy hair, a sensuous tail and somewhat staring eyes, its hands held up, palms turned towards its little mouth, that seemed to be saying "Ooohhaa". A small brown paper parcel, a Paquet Congo, which contained her baby teeth, and a handkerchief, knotted and tied; within its knots, turning to yellow dust, was her navel string.

In another paquet Congo, the one that had belonged to Ti-Pap, there was a quantity of red and black seeds

called Jumbie beads, strung together with small cowrie shells, which he had worn around his neck all his
life, it had been his talisman for luck and his amulet for
protection both charged with specific forms of psychic
force, two of his molars, and dirt from the grave that had
swallowed him.

◆ ◆ ◆

"Lapo di chapoti

Ka fè plézi;-

Lapo-mwen

Li byen poli;

É mwen ka bay plézi

Menm tout nonm gwav!"

They all sang, which may be freely rendered thus:—

"I am dimpled, young,

Round-limbed, and strong,

With sapodilla-skin

That is good to see:

All glossy-smooth

Is this skin of mine;

And the most serious of men

Like to look at me!"

This they sang to Sidoné Nathaniel's Spanish guitar. They were on a picnic at the Maraval reservoir. Huge bamboo arches whispered in the wind, blowing in a faultless sky above the rushing river; in the surrounding hills the bell birds called high noon.

"He likes you."

"Who, Eustace Bétaudier?"

"No."

"Who, Lionel Belasco?"

"No."

"Who, who?"

"Sidoné Nathaniel likes you."

"No, he is an old man."

"He still likes you."

"He was married twice."

"Perhaps he want to marry again."

The yellow-tail birds cackled out loud and made raucous love in their pendulum nests high up in the startlingly arrayed immortelles. The picnickers all sang Ma Coclise:

> "Old year's night she fetin' well
>
> Ma Coclise now sick as hell
>
> And for the doctor day have sent
>
> For to give she medicament,
>
> An' so he say when he done come:

'Gie she plenty laudanum'.

Coclise tink he saying 'Rum'

So she cryin' 'give me some

'An' Mister doctor, give me mine widout water'

"That will give Mama a stroke, he's a black man," laughed Amélie, "it's her greatest fear." "Yes, she doesn't want the family to get any darker," said Rosa, "it's bad enough already with us, already. . ." "Rosa! shhh, your mouth's too big." They laughed, falling over each other, overturning the buljol, the chicken salad and the plate of salt-fish fritters — what a thing. They all sang:

Thursday afternoon again

Ma Coclise feelin' pain.

Call Abbé to do he function

And to gie she extreme unction.

An' so he say when he done come:

In saecula saeculorum'.

Coclise tink he saying 'Rum'

So she cryin' give me some

'An Mistah Abbé give me mine widout water'.

"An Mistah Bétaudier. Ba mwen sa mwen san glo," laughed Amélie.

Sidoné Nathaniel looked at her good, thinking, she red 'till she white, he smiled in his song, she like black people, no he thought, she like Rosa Rémy, they must be like each other, he smiled into the eyes of Amélie Maximilien, I will think of you every day, he thought, I will sleep on your white linen, we will bathe together in my lakou, my yard, you and me, from the same butter-pan, with my calabash. He laughed out loud.

> Den anudder day did pass
> Ma Coclise near brede she las'
> And for lawyer dey now sent
> For to make she testament
> An' so he say when he done come:
> 'You gotta make yuh' testamentum'.
> Coclise tink he saying 'Rum'
> So she cryin' give me some
> 'An Mistah lawyer give me mine widout water'.

Amélie's glance met both his eyes, and ricocheted off and away into the direction of the yellow-tail birds, who all cackled unanimously at her discomfort. Look how red she get, thought Rosa. Look how red she get, thought Sidoné Nathaniel, as his and Rosa's eyes glanced off each other's.

She must like him, thought Rosa, smiling to herself. She must like me, thought Sidoné Nathaniel, laughing out loud.

> Sunday after midday fell
> Ma Coclise did start to smell
> And so dey call de undertaker
> Dat he might a coffin make her

An' so he say when he done come:

'At las' she gone to infernum'.

Coclise tink he saying 'Rum'

So she cryin' give me some

'An Mister Taker give me mine widout water'.

Their party broke up at the call of the François Boi-selle. The Paramin funity donkey carts were heading into Town, piled high with bunches of chive, rosemary, Spanish thyme, parsley, sage, roucou, spinach, melon-genes and big ripe tomatoes, and the picnickers were hitching a ride.

◆   ◆   ◆

He was only seen in the last quarter of the Moon.

He occupied most of what was still standing of the old slave barracks of the long abandoned La Fantaisie property that overlooked the plantation graveyard, which contained just one tomb.

He lived there in a nightmare's nest of piles of old London Graphic, parts of old boots, pieces of cow horn, snake and alligator skins, crapaud bottoms pressed flat, emitting powerful odours, aplenty of vials and bottles, containing he had no idea what, old rags, assorted feathers, several blue milk of magnesia bottles, a bag of carbide, corbeaux heads, vipers' jaws, bones of cats, a whole dog's skull, a donkey jaw bone, parrots' beaks, dogs' teeth, an entire mapapire snake floating in a bottle of formaldehyde, a live young female mapapire zanana, an elderly twenty-one foot long boa-constrictor, two deadly coral snakes that would appear from the crown of his hat, just like a Pharaoh, to terrify his customers, his victims and his patients.

He had five crocus bags of graveyard dirt that contained assorted human bones, a sealed ware jar that held the powdered remains of several puffer fish, the vital ingredient for the creation of zombis, another sealed ware jar that contained leaves of the pretty little climbing plant Mikania Guaco, the antidote for snake bite, important for the retaining of power, because only Naza knew that after taking a cup of Guaco tea, he was able to catch with impunity the most dangerous snakes, which would writhe in his bare hands as though touched by a hot iron. This inoculation gave to his perspiration the strong odour of faeces which was nauseous, but made his pet reptiles, to the amazement of all others, most disinclined to put a bite on him. You understand.

There were spectacles galore with different colour lenses, a variety of rums, plenty egg shells, several coffin handles made of brass, two brass chalices, piece of a German flag, a collection of doll's eyes, a whole ox skull with horns, plus a large quantity of cow horns, twenty or more, a great number of earthen balls, over a hundred, some small, some big, some painted blue, others white on the outside, some contained egg shells, cowrie shells, human hair and rags, tied up with vines, others contained the skulls of cats and birds' beaks, stuck round with dog and human teeth, heaps of clothes, glass beads, a human foetus floating in a big sweetie bottle, several black suits, a section of used hangman rope, thick old unread books on magic stolen from the Freemasons Lodge above Queen Street, tied up tight, and then strapped up with thick leather belts, buckled, stamped and sealed with wax, scorpions and centipedes suspended in alcohol, a big marble slab, bits of Masonic regalia, rotting rugs, what looked like a confessional box plushly upholstered in red crushed velvet, a child's coffin, new. A Fry's Chocolate Marshmallow box containing six hundred and sixty three dollars in Colonial Bank notes, and another couple of hundred dollars in copper silver and gold coins of a multitude of denominations and origins.

A human skull in excellent condition stood on a nice mahogany side table, next to a cow foot, hoof and all, standing by were two brass candle holders, two chamber pots, one enamelled with a floral pattern stamped 'Made in Engelfeld', the other quite dented, chipped and scorched, a few chairs, some pram wheels, altar cloths, two chasubles, a Superintendent's hat, and a mattress, stained with sin.

There were several left side, patent-leather high-heeled lady's shoes in assorted colours, a bridal gown from times gone by, a long, long iron chain, shackles, a violin with one string, his dead mother's old mortar with something very stink inside it, several rusty cannon balls, and a great deal more that could not possible be taken in with a casual glance.

In all that rubbish, near to a window stood an antique planter's chair, with swing-out leg rests, well upholstered, freshly varnished, occupying its own clean space on a small Persian carpet. Standing next to it, about three feet high, was a silhouette shape, cut from a one inch thick Mora plank, nicely painted to represent a grinning, old time house slave, his face, black as tar, holding a shining silver ornate serving dish upon which lay an oddly shaped, black thunder stone.

He lay on the mattress stained with sin and gazed at the planter's chair. It was bathed in moonlight, beautiful to behold. As he stared, the moon seemed to shine brighter, the varnished arms and sides gleamed, the heavily brocaded upholstery appeared to deepen, the thick carved legs seemed to grow majestic, the chair to recline invitingly, the silver ornate serving dish flashed a phosphorescent white glow that lit him and the cluttered room; in contrast, the black thunder stone that lay at its centre appeared to attract, to absorb the light, becoming more dense, more black, more heavy. The Baron Samedi's chair. His stone.

He knew the law. He knew that it is man, he, himself, that makes the Magic, not the gods, not the Loa; he had to find the trick to make the Magic that makes the luck, his luck. He it was who set the powerful forces in motion, he, himself, by the force of his will, draws the zombi from the grave. His master was Baron Samedi; the zombi, the spirit of the dead, the soulless person and the black thunder stone, they were all one and the same.

He sang softly to himself as if in someone else's voice in a fine tenor, the moonlight now even brighter ". . . I want to have that woman. Don't let she go, Lord Executor, hold on to that woman. Don't let she go . . ." As he sang, he felt the transformation commence. He felt it in his face, he felt his skin harden and fold, his jaw protrude, his gums painful as his teeth grew and changed the shape of his mouth and head; suddenly his back hunched, his eyes saw differently, he snorted, his nose and mouth full of spit, his hands were changing, he saw black bristles appear, he was crouching on the mattress on all fours, he honked and snorted like a pig.

He was perfectly clear in is mind, he started to sing the song of the grave digger, an eerie jerky dirge, he felt his sex grow huge. He wanted her, the red one. The friend. He snorted and rubbed his snout along the mattress, up and down, on this side, that side. He saw when the Baron Samedi, the lord of the graveyard, his master, assumed his place in the antique planter's chair like a lord, a king of the underworld. He ran from the barrack, rutting, his snout to the ground, his sex painful. That was the night that he entered the Doctor's house and climbed upon the red one.

He now had another one, a yellow one. He had turned her, she is now his, they will think she dead, she dead, she dead. He sat back in the antique planter's chair and looked out on the graveyard, the old man's, Zinga's grave, the béké's tomb. "He, a Baron too, a white people Baron, me a Baron, a Guinée Baron." He drank from a bottle of Cecil Marquis rum. "Aahhh! Tomorrow night she coming home, Marie-Aurélie, you go wake up on that mattress, then is me and you." He snorted like a pig. He never returned to his nightmare's nest, but instead took up residence where the Court had sentenced him, not too far away from La Fantaisie Road at the newly-opened asylum for the mentally disturbed at Sainte-Anne.

◆　◆　◆

On Holy Thursday, in the lurching carriage, traveling first class, she sat, in high-necked white cotton trimmed with small crochet, a brightly-coloured waistband relieving the starchiness. Her hair, bright red in the morning sunlight, was piled up round and around her head, her hat impaled with long shiny pins. Her lovely hands, restless, her big nose, freckled, her bright blue eyes alight with excitement. Thirty-nine years old, a rather attractive, full-breasted woman, tall, a good size bottom, she was on her way to meet a man in San Fernando.

I could imagine the bustle of the railway station, not the present one that we know well, but a previous building, smaller, with the older trains. The smell in the railway station was one of red-hot coals, axle grease, iron and steel, horse apples and copra, coconut oil mixed with freshly bagged cocoa beans; a swelter of politeness, of "au revoirs", "good mornings", "adieus", "beg your pardons", "will you just let me." People dressed differently: the Patois-speaking women of colour tied their heads to indicate status in an esoteric language understood amongst themselves. Other women wore corsets, long dresses down to their ankles and laced-up boots and large before-the-turn-of-the-century hats. Hats, cork hats, feathered hats, felt hats, parasols; old Mr. Popplewell's grandfather, the ticket collector; smartly turned-out police constables, white cork-hats, the freshly arrived Indians, nearly naked, emaciated, skin and bone, burnt black, carrying enormous bundles, boxes, suitcases on their heads, eyes rolling in faces with near-death expressions; Scottish boiler-makers going and coming, lost turns of phrase, "Palé pa wimèd, ma chè." "Pawòl pa tini koulè." "Pawòl pa tini koulè", the clang of steel on steel, green flags, red flags, whistles, the rush of steam on the sidings, an enormous Négresse emerging from it, followed by a column of little jet-black girls, each identical and identically dressed, be-ribboned in blue and red; white people, the local béké, now popularly referred to by American travel writers as the 'French Creoles'; the English people, with pith helmets and spine shields, with wicker luggage and black Bajan liveried chauffeurs, bowing and scraping and kissing their asses, and scornfully disdainful to all else.

Late nineteenth century Port-of-Spain, as it was now referred to by nearly everyone, was full of horses, donkeys carts and mule-trams. Iron-wheeled traffic. New buildings, fountains, shady parks; no one had been decapitated, flogged to death, burnt or hung in public for almost sixty years.

Sidoné Nathaniel met her at the station in San Fernando, they stayed chastely in separate rooms at a guesthouse on High Street. The next day, they set out on the steamer, the 'Lady Harris', for Cedros. She had not known a man before him. Her circle of friends were Rosa Rémy's friends and a cousin of the Maximilien family, Felicity Negretti, called Auntie Pinky, a beautiful old woman with too much pink make-up that made her look like an opera singer.

Amélie came to know Sidoné Nathaniel over some five or six years. He had courted her with ribald songs, sicreé figs, corny jokes, and a great deal of loving attention. He was a fine-featured man, a dark-skinned Marabou, one could guess, five eighths African, with the rest French. His grandfather on his father's side was a Frenchman, Philémon de Goulart. On his mother's side as well he had French forebears, far back in time, on another island. Once well-off affranchis, Free Blacks, they migrated to Trinidad, bringing with them slaves and acquiring cane estates in the Naparimas. He owned lands in Mayaro and a house in Port-of-Spain, on Belmont Circular Road. He was tall, over six feet, dressed stylishly, carried a cane, had strong arms and shoulders, upright in bearing, was a good horseman, and had very nice manners.

"I will not marry you, Sidoné."

"Why?"

"I have my reasons."

"I know your reasons, or reason."

"And what is that?"

"Because I am black. And you are white, or look white, because your father is Dr. Maximilien, and your mother is a great French lady."

"No, Sidoné, that is not the reason." She looked at him. Since that day in Maraval he had not left her thoughts, or if he did, he had not wandered far. She liked him. He made her laugh when they were together, in company of Rosa's friends, it was always better when he was there. Rosa liked him. Rosa said to her, he wants you Amé, she answered that she knew what he wanted. Rosa agreed, yes, but he wants you, perhaps he loves you. Could you love him, she asked. Amé denied that, with many no, no, no's, and kissed Rosa, with love, and yes, passion. He is a dear man. I know that.

"Sidoné. I, Rosa and I . . ."

"I know, you are 'les amies'."

"No Sidoné. What we are is, . . . is massissi, lovers, we have been lovers from the time we were girls. I love her. We have a life, we have been through many trials, more than you can imagine. And yes, my family, it would be a scandal, but I am scandalous already."

"Spend time with me, Amé, come down to Cedros for the Easter holidays."

She was compelled to laugh. Two weeks in Cedros with you! But he persisted. La Sirène Rosa encouraged, and she said yes.

He behaved towards her, from when they first met, and continued to do so for years, even after they had married, as though she was a person superior to him;

because of her psychic abilities and her lineage, both black and white. His was, however, not a deferential manner, for he took possession of her and commanded her passions, won her trust, and yes, love.

I have a mental picture of Amélie Nathaniel, my grandmother, that Easter weekend, reclining on a curved-backwards-by-the-wind coconut tree, her white dress sharp against a sepia-toned, dotted, slow-moving picture, ravished by the wind, the sea, the sky, and Sidoné, my grandfather. She said she loved him for sixteen years, and "Granville was the best years of my life".

Granville estate, Cedros, of which he was the manager, was remote, almost in Venezuela; it was more than two thousand acres and stretched from the Columbus channel on the South-Western peninsula of the island to the Gulf of Paria. It was almost a day's journey from Port-of-Spain by boat, which only went there twice a month in a manner not dissimilar to Humphrey Bogart and Katharine Hepburn in the film 'African Queen'. Another way was by train, which went to San Fernando and onwards as far as Princes Town, and then by ox-cart to Granville estate.

It was a vast coconut and cocoa plantation that belonged to the Maynards, an English family who came out to Trinidad in the 1850s to take advantage of the losses incurred by the original French settlers as a result of the emancipation of the slaves in 1834. In a tall wooden house they lived, which stood on a hill, surrounded by coconut trees as far as the eye could see, the crisscrossing "Xs" of their trunks, the bushy green canopy bulging with nuts. The peaceful solitude, the wind forever rushing, lamp-lit evenings, singing songs to his Spanish guitar. The wooden house bare of paint and hardly any furniture, was only made domestic by her white crochet and starched linens. Early mornings, the silence of her solitude went for weeks. He would be gone on horse-back, a big, broad-brimmed khaki felt hat pinned up on one side like an Australian trooper. They were married in 1874. He was a member of the Mayaro Road Board, a forest ranger for the Department of Agriculture, and estate manager for Archibald Maynard Esq.

Little Sidoné was conceived there. They moved to the house in Belmont opposite the convent of the Carmel-ite Sisters at the foot of Hermitage Road for the con-finement. La Sirène Rosa was the mid-wife.

◆　◆　◆

After the return to France of Claude-Ambrose du Vivier de Noailles and his wife and children, and the passing away of Tanti Cyrillia, La Sirène Rosa sold the properties on George Street to an Italian businessman by the name of Antonmattei, and leased the abattoir and the lands on which it stood, on the South-Eastern edge of the Town, to Alfonso Rumazo Vizcardo, a Venezuelan who had just managed to escape the ongoing military and civil depredations of that unfortunate Republic, choosing instead to settle in the civilised safety of Brit-ish colonial Trinidad. She was, in fact, very well off.

To be close to Amélie, she acquired a parcel of land on Rudin Lane, which bounded with where Amé and Sidoné lived on the Belmont Circular Road, and built a charming cottage there for herself. Her garden overflowed with flowering blooms and a vast variety of medicinal plants, herbs, roots and shrubs, a veritable herbarium of worm grass, cocolicka, shandilé, rachette, géritout, zèbapique, dité payee, marigold, vervine, mayoc chapelle and grain amba feuille, seed under leaf.

Their sexual intimacy, postponed, faded with Amélie's marriage to Sidoné, and with Rosa's interest diverted to other concerns and to other partners. The original bonds of trust and love, which had been forged by the shared perils, emergencies and enemies that they had faced, which had cemented their friendship in the first place, only deepened as life went by. In fact, their relationship became more complex. This was the case because of their combined mental and psychic capacities, their natural empathy and indeed sympathy for the poor people who lived amongst them. They were what is called 'Quimboiseurs' in the French islands, traditional healers, dispensers of ancient remedies and ritual consultants. Customs and habits formed, superstitions maintained, the ways of the eighteenth century lingered well into the nineteenth, the common people were needy, some desperate and sick, both mentally and physically, they came to them for the care and the comfort that they understood and trusted.

Amélie and La Sirène Rosa saw, every Saturday, dozens of people in Amélie's L-shaped front gallery. Some came for prayers, which were handed out on slips of paper, with instructions on when and how they should be uttered and in which combinations of the orthodox and recognised Catholic ones they may be applied. These were often directed to the Order of Archangels who ruled and inhabited the World of Formation, and were addressed directly to Metatron and Michael, Gabriel and Raphael, but there were also the lesser know angelic powers to whom appeals were made such as Iameth, the angel encountered in occult and apocryphal endeavours, who was the beneficent power that could overthrow the machinations of the Kunospaston, the deamon of the sea. Mothers, wives and sweethearts of sailors and fishermen would arrive on Saint Peter's day to acquire, enhance and or revitalise charms and amulets against the dangers of the deep. Then there was Iachadiel, an angel whose name is found inscribed on the fifth pentacle of the moon. He "serveth unto destruction and loss . . . thou mayest call upon him against all Phantoms of the night and to summon the souls of the departed from Hades". This was very popular.

Others came to experience the application of a device that generated an electric current without having any notion of what it was: operated by the turning of a handle that, when applied through wires and electrodes to the patient's temples, elbow, wrist, abdomen, bottom or privates, it could cure or bring a temporary alleviation to arthritis, rheumatic pains, neuralgia, muscular spasms, sprains and gas pains. It was also used to inaugurate treatments for spirit possession, the constant preoccupation with illusions, and to deal with the mild insanities that the combination of malnutrition and poverty could bring on. They came for electric shocks, and paid 60 cents for that.

Some came for prescriptions for herbal remedies and general advice; to strengthen a weak bladder, take slices of young green soursop, with skin and seeds, boil thoroughly, drink as a tea twice daily. Or, for the same ailment, take crushed sapodilla seeds, make a tea, this is good for stoppage of water. Painful menstruation? Try a hot glass of stout swizzled with aloes juice. Menopause? Take a treatment of charcoal powder, aloes and molasses. Kidney problems; well, slice a large melongene with its skin attached and soak it in rainwater for three days; drink a glass full of this for one week, let three days pass and repeat course. For those with lung problems engendered from smoking the foul-smelling tobacco imported from down the Main; try honey, the white of an egg and aloes.

A great many came for matters of the heart, some were desperate, others lovelorn and depressed, some had been left in the lurch, others at the church, some were in pursuit of vengeance, while others were ambitious, some sought to ascertain what their partners, spouses, fiancés, parents or offspring were up to, some sought to prevent their partners from discovering their own trespasses, while many came to talk to the dead, and many more to influence the living.

There were a few who came by appointment to consult both Amélie and La Sirène Rosa in private. This would necessitate my grandmother Amélie assuming the role of the femme-dormeuse. These séances were conducted in a little room that may have been at one time a dressing room and contained just a bentwood rocking chair, a piano-stool and a cot. Amélie would sit on the rocker, La Sirène Rosa on the piano-stool and the visitor would lay down and relax on the cot. La Sirène Rosa would encourage the visitor to be calm and to say what came to mind. After much talk the real purpose for the séance would be expressed and be agreed by all three, then La Sirène Rosa would advise the visitor to be very quiet and still. She would then encourage Amélie with gentle words to lie back in the rocking chair, close her eyes and see. She, appearing to be sleeping, would be slipping gently into a trance, and with the quiet prompting of La Sirène Rosa, Amélie would travel into the astral spheres for insights and guidance from the spirits and saints, powers and beings who dwell there. These invocations were always conducted in privacy and in secrecy, the visitor warned, and sworn to silence.

◆ ◆ ◆

7. La Sirène Rosa:-

NONM MÒ; ZÈB KA LÉVÉ DOUVAN LAPÒT-LI.
The man has died, grass grows before his door.

"So, Naza, that wretch, he is still in Sainte-Anne mad-house?"

"Yes, I hear he still counting, every time they give him a plate of food, he have to count all the rice before he eat it, you ever hear more?"

They were sitting on La Sirène Rosa's back step shelling pigeon peas and enjoying a glass of Green Chartreuse liqueur.

"And you saw the Spanish priest in your vision Amé?"

"No, I didn't see him, I just heard the caution to the spell he was using, or trying to use, to banish the souk-ounyan daemon, it was spoken softly in a woman's voice in a strange language. It came to me that it was Arabic, I thought that at the time, I don't know Arabic of course, but when I dream I understand all sorts of things that I have no knowledge of normally. I think the woman in cautioning him said something like '. . . this spirit gives unto you the knowledge of the devils, those that take to the air and are of fire and are in lust for blood, but

I counsel you,' and this was where the voice became stern, 'not to avail yourself of his services, for he is a very wicked spirit and a deceiver, who will do all in his power to entrap you and afterwards he will mock you, this is his character.' Then I heard the priest, he was frightened, begging, appealing to a spirit of virtue, saying 'you who hath preserved our forefathers from their enemies, rendering them formidable unto them so as to put them to flight, give me the answer to conquer this daemon of blood and fire and flight'. Then he said a long prayer in Latin to Saint Michael the Archangel. I heard something pour out on the ground. I saw it was grains of something. 'By this mark,' said the woman's voice, 'you will command the wicked one, the one that is in possession of the servant, to gather and to count.' I then saw the vever, the symbol in the air, 'In this seal there it is taught how the wicked is brought low, and the skinless is compelled to count and number this grain from generation to generation'; then the woman said, 'the server of the daemon is the son of the server of the daemon'.

"That's when I understood that Naza was the son of the old man, the poisoner, and that he, Naza, had inherited the curse put upon his mother, the Hololo soukounyan of long ago, the one they called Desirée. That's what I told you. The priest had trapped her with a one hundred pound bag of Guyanese rice, she had picked up nearly all, the sun had come up when they found her by the bridge on Cascade Road, unfortunately her skin was still in the mortar under the bed at home. Any grain would do, I told you, remember, and you got seed under leaf, grain amba feuille, and put it in Marie-Aurélie's coffin. How come?"

"It's all I had in the yard, I couldn't get a hundred pound bag of rice. So, the old poisoner didn't know that he had made a child with Desirée, which is a great name for a soukounyan, and that the child, the boy who came to him, to be his apprentice, was his own son, Naza?" asked La Sirène Rosa.

"No."

"And Naza didn't know that he had inherited the curse of counting seeds from his soukounyan mother Desirée?"

"No."

"Makak pa konnèt ki bwa monté!"

"No," said Amélie, "the monkey didn't know which tree to climb, this time. And talking about monkeys. Antoine Paseau died, but not by magic."

"I know," said La Sirène Rosa, "people always said it was me who straightened him out."

"This was another thing that I understood from the dream, Naza was giving him 'devil's trumpet,' datura, he was hallucinating at the end, it was the overdose datura that killed him. Hell of a thing eh? But, Rosa, what about Marie-Aurélie, what became of her?"

"She went to Gran Couva, her mother Eloïde has family there, the du Près, she now is working for the de la Rochefoucaulds, they have a big estate, she's minding the children."

"They are so poteau d'église, if they only knew that she has her death certificate in her handbag, they'd die."

As late afternoon lingered they sang:

"Mwen désann Port-d'Espagne

Achté Dobannes

Aulié sé Dobannes

Sé yon bèl-bwa mwen mennen monté!"

"Remember that one?"

"How does it go in English?"

"I went down to Port-of-Spain to buy Dobannes: instead of the Dobannes, 'tis a pretty tree—a charming girl—I bring back with me."

"What is Dobannes, Rosa?"

"Pakonnèt, ma chè, don't know, but I know what a bèl-bwa is—a charming girl . . ."

"Like you!" they both said, laughing, and pointing their fingers at each other.

That's when they saw a figure of what appeared to be a girlchild run past the wicker fence and into Amélie's back garden. La Sirène Rosa jumped up and started quickly round the other side of the house.

The little figure struggled for a moment, then went almost limp in La Sirène Rosa's grip.

"What are you doing in my lakou, eh, why you in my yard, eh?"

Looking into the face of her captive she at once realised that this was no girl, but a small person, a dwarf woman, with short limbs, stubby fingers, a large head and a pathetic expression in her watery eyes.

"Who you?. . .What you want?"

Still, the pathetic eyes stared at her.

"Amélie, call Fitzroy, tell him to go to the station, tell him to say we find somebody in the yard, tell them to come."

"Mercy, Mercy, me.. . ."

"Well, talk girl, who are you, what you want?"

"Who sent you?" asked Amélie, stooping down before the little figure.

"Tell me."

"Mercy is me, I is Mercy Miss," said the little woman in a Barbadian accent. "My mother is Fennargar the woman who is sell chatoigne by the Orphanage yonder, she send Mercy to say she wants the lady with the vision to come see she, she froighten to come sheself so she sen' me, Mercy."

"Why is she frightened, Mercy?"

"She na want no one see she here, she 'fraid, Miss."

Amélie looked into the face of desperation, confusion, yes, and fear?

"What is she, you, so afraid of, Mercy, that she can't come to see me like everybody else, and you, instead of coming to the front gate and calling, you running around to the back, why, were you going to do something? Or leave something, come tell me."

"Me mudder sen to give you dis."

The little woman took from her blouse a square envelope, on it was written in an elaborate script the words "To La Reine Rosa".

"Where did you get that?"

"Rosa, be careful, she's small."

"It's a letter, it's addressed to me, Amé, it's from a priest, an Abbé Carondelet of Mayaro. Your mother gave you this for me?"

"Yes Miss."

"How she get it?"

"Miss Gouilière bring it."

"Why didn't you bring it for me?"

"I was bringin it, Miss, but Miss Gouilière say put it in the door."

◆　◆　◆

That evening over a great steaming meal of chicken and pork pelau served with a fiery venison stew, fried plantains and zaboka, Sidoné said, "That's the parish priest at Mayaro, Abbé Carondelet. I met him when I went to see Amadé Frontin, remember, I told you about him. Amadé and André Joachim didn't have too many good words to say about him, this is a great pelau, Rosa."

"Thank you Sidoné. But tell me, who are the Gouilières?"

"Mayaro people. Losea Gouilière received a land grant in Governor Chacón's time. He had a son with Mayotte Veronique, he was living with her in a house on Radix point. The son, I think his name was Carmélite, he left Mayaro, went somewhere and came back, with two children, little girls, Dabéline and Elézèth, I don't know what became of them. What the priest is saying is that there is a great monster, an evil that he has no understanding of, 'soukounyan' he say, sounds so to me! You say this letter came to Fennargar, the Bajan woman, the chataigne lady, how did you come by it?"

"A dwarf brought it."

"Yes, we were shelling the peas when I saw this person in the yard. It gave us a fright, we had just been talking about 'you know who' when I saw something pass by the gate, strange."

"Her name is Mercy, if you see her, high so with hat."

"Go and see Fennargar, it is something of a coincidence, though, I have to go to Mayaro next month, there is to be a meeting on the road extension, suddenly everybody have a piece of land right where the road is passing. See Fennargar, that should be amusing."

The following morning La Sirène Rosa attended Holy Mass at six o'clock at the new Saint François church on Belmont Circular Road, and after Mass took a walk up Layan Hill in hope of finding Fennargar.

A dirt track took over after a few hundred feet from the paved roadway that took the hill with a leap and entered a forest of mango trees, cool and breezy in the morning light. Not far along she saw a little house painted blue with white trim, there was an abundance of chickens, ducks and turkeys in the yard and five 'gouti dogs tied, all barking, below a fowl coop under a big chataigne tree.

"Bon jour, bon jour, good morning," she called. "Anyone home?"

"Morning, eh, eh, Miss Rémy, you came, come inside, no, wait, give me a chance to fix up." She could be heard waking up someone.

"Come get up, Miss Rémy has come to see me—ah coming now, Miss Rémy!"

Two young fellows, dishevelled, eyes still full of sleep, could be seen stumbling around the cottage's front room.

"It's all right, Fennargar, it's early, I have time, we just have to chat for a moment."

They sat in a tidy little front room, Mercy had made coffee, and La Sirène Rosa was glad to share the piping hot plate of pumpkin fritters that seemed to replenish themselves miraculously.

"So, Elézèth Gouilière is your husband's sister in law and she lives in Mayaro."

"Yes, she's living with Glenford Timothy in Saint Zuliere Road. She brought the letter. She and the priest, well, they're close, you understand, she washes, cleans, cooks and irons for him."

"Yes, I understand, did she tell you why he, as a priest, an Abbé, would want to meet me, of all people?"

"Water must be more than flour, Miss Rémy. You know Mayaro? It's far you know, it closer to Barbados than to Town, the people there are . . ." She searched for the word.

"Superstitious?"

"Yes, thank you Miss Rémy, we don't have all that at Drax Hall, we are Christians in Barbados. I am Methodist myself, we know duppies and steel donkey, long ago stories to fool ignorant people, foolishness. We don't have anything like that, all that fire."

They were looking at a sketch made by the Abbé at the bottom of his letter.

"Yes, well, we have that here, I haven't heard of that for a long time," she paused, the words, 'we talked about that daemon yesterday,' crossed her mind quite clearly, almost as though someone had spoken them, she felt a pang. But continued, "in Trinidad it's different, there is a different culture here, different people came here from different parts of the world, there was a mix up, a callaloo, of everything, you know. We must have faith in God ma chère." She took her both hands, "The Word was made Flesh and dwelt amongst us."

"Yes, Amen, Miss Rémy, but this has fire, look."

The Abbé Carondelet's letter, addressed to La Reine Rosa, was, to say the least, very respectful. It explained that there had been a quantity of particularly bloody killings on the estates and in Mayaro village itself. 'Macabre' he had written, 'grotesque, horrific, and shocking'. He had notified the Archdiocese, as this was plainly the work of the Devil, Satan was walking abroad, a Vampire, as he understood it, had made its presence known and taken over. He wrote that the person who saw after the presbytery had described this evil which he had sketched. It showed a very ugly old woman peeling away what appeared to be her skin, then depositing it in a wooden mortar and transforming herself into a fiery ball, next to an open window.

He wrote that the people said that this was a soukounyan. The letter closed by asking if she, La Sirène Rosa, had any advice or information that could explain this aberration, and that he would be grateful if he heard from her, and naturally he hoped that his letter would be treated with the greatest confidentiality, as he was doing this, writing to her, because the parishioners had begged him to, especially after the two Irish priests sent by the Archdiocese had left after just a month without demonstrating any success. In truth, things had gone from very bad to terrifying. The villages were living in fear, particularly after Madame Fournillière of Bon Séjour estate had been found dead in her bed, blood leading to an open window. He had been approached by the planters in private, who advised that if only for the sake of giving comfort to the villagers, he should put himself at the disposal of Mlle Rosa Rémy, and this being the case, he had written to her as a last resort, that too must be kept confidential, for the obvious reasons.

"Well, thank you, Fennargar, these fritters, I don't think that I have ever tasted better," said La Sirène Rosa, rising.

"Look your hat, Miss Rémy."

"Merci, Mercy, thank you for the fritters."

"You will help them, Miss Rémy?"

"I don't know if I can, these things sometimes pass away after the reason for their appearance has been made known, or the purposes they serve have been achieved, I don't know. Au revoir, Fennargar."

"Elézèth is coming to Town next month, would you receive her if I told her to come and see you?"

"Yes of course. Au revoir."

◆ ◆ ◆

Elézèth was a good-looking, dark-skinned person whose features suggested Carib forebears. Perhaps forty, she was a tall, strapping, becoming buxom woman, at first shy, especially in the presence of Sidoné Nathaniel, where she was reduced to speechlessness, incapable of looking at him in the face, at first.

"We need to get her to tell us everything, Rosa."

"Well, there is an old remedy for reticence. It goes; pick a lily in June under the waning moon, moisten it with laurel juice and bury it in dung; worms will breed, dry them and scatter on the person's pillow. And she will talk in her sleep and all."

"Where did you get that from?"

"Oh, I read that the toad is the third of Beelzebub's seventy-two spirits, Billifares, who appears as a great black-headed toad—he is the opposite of the good spirit Vassago. The spell means that Billifares is to be compelled to make her talk in her sleep."

"Rosa, you have been reading Naza's books on magic, books he couldn't read himself."

"Well, I hate to see books thrown away, and I have an interest in the subject. On that one I took a note," she said, rummaging in her handbag, "Yes, let's see, 'The lily in June under a waning moon', we are informed, 'means Lilith Queen Night under the influence of the daemon Shimri; the laurel is the Raven of Dispersion, Q'areb Zarag'."

"OH! Rosa, that sounds awful!"

"You never can tell when this sort of information will come in useful."

"I hope it never does."

There was no need for spells. Alone with La Sirène Rosa and Amélie, Elézèth became loquacious and funny, and after a while, with a little encouragement, Amélie had charmed her and made a lovely lunch for everyone on Whit Monday, when they had all a little too much sangria and black cake, she told hilarious stories of long ago in Mayaro.

On the train to Sangre Grande, whence they would travel by cart to Manzanilla, and thence in the same manner to Mayaro, on the following day; La Sirène Rosa, Amélie and Elézèth Gouilière sat together, the cane-covered countryside rushing by to the clang and whistle of the train. La Sirène Rosa broached the subject which was the reason for their visit to the Bande-de-l'Est, as the East coast was called in those days.

"So Elézèth, tell me about the Abbé, is he a nice person?"

"Oh yes, Miss Rosa, he well good for himself, the first day he reach I see he size me up good, ah watch him, he name man, he look like to me."

"And, he name man for true?" asked Amélie.

"What! If I tell you, some days I have to run and hide, he like black woman too bad, but he making confusion in the parish."

"How is that?"

"Well, Miss Rosa, everybody does do their business to suit they selves. If a man living with a woman, donkey years, and they have children, and everything good, Father Carondelet have no right to interfere, I tell him, 'you have no right interfering, what you telling people that they living in sin for, that's their concern, their business.' He went, he tell Clarise Frontin to say she want to get married, well the next thing Clarise get one cut tail, he is too farce, then he find out that she and Amadé is family, they have the same name, well that make everything worse, he want to know who is he father who is she mother, he too farce, people don't like that."

"He sounds like a hypocrite to me."

"Well, he mean well, but he name man."

"When did this thing start, the deaths?"

"Since year before last, before Father Carondelet came. Edwina Nelson, Athelstan daughter, take een, she get thin, all she face bruise, she arm, she body, ah watch she bathing, ah say like she get licks, the next thing they find her dead one morning in the cocoa, quite down by Maloney. Miss Timothy say she never see a person who look so bad dead. Then the Grenadian girl, who was living with the policeman, he come home ah Sunday, the horse wouldn't go in the yard, he stand up outside, sweating, the boy run inside, blood all over the place, she dead in the bed, she neck open."

"A report was made?"

"OH yes! Monsieur Alphonse come, the police inspector from Sangre Grande, the Sergeant, everybody, they talk, they talk, then they left. The next morning they find the Indian boy, Sammy, dead, like something bite him and drain him. After Father Carondelet came, everything calm down. He went to everybody, he talk to everybody, we hold a procession on Corpus Christi day from the church to Maloney. They gave a thanks-giving, he make everybody say the chaplet, every house, every night. Well you know some people not in that. He say he want to hear confession from everybody in the parish, everybody must go to holy communion every Sunday, well, that is another thing."

"But the prayers and a better religious life helped, didn't it?"

"No, Miss Rosa, Diamond son get kill same way."

"How many people have died, Elézèth?"

"Miss Rosa, eleven people meet their death, it too dangerous to go out in the night, people sleeping with their house lock up tight. Father Carondelet get frighten, one evening I just shutting up the office, I see he come, he pale. 'What happen?' I ask him. 'The Devil is walking abroad, Elézèth,' he tell me, he shaking. The next morning they find the old white lady dead in she bed. Well, after Father went, Monsieur Alphonse reach, that was his family, he say they bringing a person from Martinique, some man, the man come, he spend the night walking up and down the village, they find him next morning, the thing take off his skin from his back, Miss Rosa, he was white as a sheet, I never see more. The two priest leave that same morning, Monsieur Alphonse give André Joachim, Evan Popwell, Amadé Frontin guns, they say he mounted them with silver bullets, he is the Warden. Old Mally she put rice by she door, next day the rice gone, they find Mally in the churchyard, she neck pop. A big gash in she neck, right here."

"Who is this fiend, Elézèth, who doing this?" asked Amélie. "Do you know, do you have any idea?"

"No, Miss Amé, nobody know."

"Or want to know."

"Since you living there, Elézèth, any new people come to the village, or to the estates, strangers, you know people who don't join in, mix, you know?"

"No, Miss Amé, people don't come to Mayaro."

Sidoné Nathaniel's house at the end of Church Road overlooked the Atlantic Ocean. It received the Trade Winds that poured like an invisible torrent out of the sunrise, constantly harassing, and putting into perpetual disarray the branches of the million and one coconut trees that lined the Eastern shore for almost thirty miles. The wind took one's breath away, and hurled spoken words, whispered promises, ancient secrets and fervent prayers skyward to become lost in realms of scattered dreams on an ongoing basis.

"Sidoné, you're not afraid of the soukounyan, you going to walk on the beach, at this hour?"

"No ma chè, soukounyan stories are not on my cloud. It's a lovely night; I think I will walk down to Rajeunir estate and see if André Joachim is there."

She didn't hear him come in and only became aware of him when she awoke with a shout.

"You alright Amé, calm down ma chè, it's all right, everything is alright, what happen eh. . . have a sip, good, good."

It had been an outstanding dream that had achieved a super-real quality that could only be appreciated by cinemagoers in the late twentieth century when three-dimensional cinematography had been perfected.

"What did you dream, Amé, what was it, tell me, tell me, if only to get it over with, come, come."

She had curled herself into a ball that fitted snugly from beneath his chin to his slightly bent knees. With her face buried in an armpit, she shook her head. No, he thought, you can't say a word tonight. "Shhh, it's alright, go to sleep, it's alright."

But it was not alright. About half an hour later, just as he was about to drift off to sleep, she was awake again, gasping for breath, her face white, drained of colour, her red hair actually standing out on end, her neck and shoulders out of her nightgown as though she had emerged from it.

"Amé, my God, what is it? Come get up, let me, there, put this around you, come stand by the window to catch your breath."

"No, no, you stay, come back here, I feel claustrophobic, call Rosa, no don't take the lamp, go quick, go quick."

They sat on the bed, the three of them. Three pitch oil lamps illuminated the bedroom, the two windows that opened on to the beach had been closed and barred.

"Rosa, I saw it, I saw it, my God, Rosa, we have to go, we have to leave here, we have to go. Sidoné."

According to Amé she had fallen to sleep soon after he had left her. No sooner had she slipped into sleep, she saw him, Sidoné, walking on the beach in the pitch black, above were stars in multitudes, she noticed, 'how beautiful' she said, in the dream. That was when she saw one star come falling out of the sky. With a fright she saw that it was not a star at all, but a rolling ball of blazing fire, transparent, throbbing, emitting waves of heat; she said she saw him, Sidoné, stop and look as though he was seeing something go by. The ball of fire came towards her, she could see inside it, there was a person, a face, consumed in fire, burning like a living coal, red and black, a hideous face, a face in agony, burning.

"It was hideous. That's when I woke up."

"You saw a face in that thing?"

"Yes, yes, inside of it, it was blazing all around. I felt claustrophobic, I felt that I could not breathe, it was so real, it came to me, the fireball with a daemon in it at a speed."

"That was the first dream?"

"Yes, the next dream, now, that was me, I saw myself sleeping there next to Sidoné, then this person was in the room, a woman, she hold me, look," she showed them her skin on her shoulders, they were red and bruised.

"OH! Bondyé, Amé."

"It had come for me, the face . . . the face."

The night, or what remained of it, passed slowly for the three, with the sound of thunder rumbling somewhere, and a silence that Rosa realised was as a result of a sudden cessation of the wind.

As morning appeared, strange and reluctant behind an ominous sky of the darkest grey imaginable, a heat, damp and breathless, caused a sweat to rise and an incipient headache to commence behind her eyes. She was just about to go inside from the side gallery where she had sought rest and a time to think, when she saw coming through the coconut trees a person, a woman, who came to the gate.

"Morning, I come to Miss Rémy?"

"Yes, it is I."

"Miss Rémy, I is Dabéline Gouilière, Elézèth sister, I come to talk to you now."

"Yes, push the gate, come."

"Miss Rémy, I coming to you for you to save me, you are the only person who can save me. Please."

"Come sit down, would like a cup of coffee?"

"No thanks, Miss Rémy, I just want to tell you everything."

La Sirène Rosa looked well at the person who sat before her in the half-light of dawn. She saw a face, dark, hard-lined, thin-lipped; the woman's head was tied in a red and black madras turban, her black dress was stiff with dirt and stained and scorched, her bandaged feet bloody. There were traces of blood in the saliva in the corners of her mouth, she swallowed with difficulty as if her throat was swollen, her eyes were purulent and blood-shot, and could not meet her own, her teeth were large, out of proportion, puss was oozing from one ear, and there was a heat that came from her, strong, with a strong smell of hot coals. She shook, in little spasms, her knees and hands trembled. There was a sense of something strong and violent, dangerous, just barely under control. Like an animal leashed and brought to heel.

Dabéline's story, told in a whisper in the gathering storm, frightened her, causing a reeling feeling of desperate panic, her heart beat so fast she could hear it in her ears. She could hardly sit to listen. She felt her stomach grip upon itself, her mouth filled with saliva, she retched and had to stand at the gallery's rail, a cold sweat enveloped her, she shook her head and looked up at the rushing clouds to fight off dizziness and a feeling of being trapped in a cycle whose origins wound themselves back over centuries. This is old and bad, these are the angels of darkness, she said to herself. This is not Naza and his evil-minded tricks, this is hell, this woman has become a servant to daemons.

"Amé, this is old, old Nigromancy, the angels of darkness from the rebellion and fall of the evil one, Lucifer, have sent spirits to take possession. She, Dabéline, is the soukounyan's vehicle, we have to find the power behind this and either kill them both, or exorcise it. Or it will kill us."

"Exorcise? That priest can't exorcise Dabéline. Is she the soukounyan?"

"No, and yes, the soukounyan daemon takes over Dabéline every night, she was seduced into a relationship with a Geneviève Gauzhelm when she came to Mayaro twenty, thirty years ago with her father and her sister Elézèth from Saint Vincent. She was taken in by this old white woman as a child, to be her companion, a helper. At first everything was fine; then the old woman revealed herself as a power that could make her every wish come true; she had success with men, she got money, the land at Radix Point. Everything."

"And the sister Elézèth, is she. . .?"

"No, she is poteau d'église: the church, the Abbé, is her concern. It was Dabéline who became the servant of the soukounyan daemon: she had an initiation which sounds to me like alchemy, where after concocting something vile from the body parts of a corpse, a copper penny is used to extract the liver, an oil is processed. But it's more than that; that is the outer form, this is a fusion of Vampire traditions. The power to externally transform the self into a receptacle is associated with transmogrification, this the work of the spirit Aratron, it has to with the creation of the souls of men, and what they really are; also their estate after death. A form of black magic coming from Europe, white people's black magic meeting the same sort of thing out of Africa.

"What Dabéline tried to explain, as I understand her, is that the Gauzhelm family were Courlanders originally, people from Tobago, who came to Mayaro long, long ago in early Spanish times, they had to run from the people in Tobago, they are the oldest family here. From what I could understand from her, they brought with them a Vampire witchcraft cult. A woman in that family, perhaps a hundred years ago, or more, became familiar with an African slave on their estate, a man who was possessed by a Sasabonsam, a Vampire-like Jumbie out of Africa. She said something about Ashanti in Ghana, she has no idea what she is saying, she's uneducated, she is just repeating what she has heard; she say it is the African variety of the Vampire, it has iron teeth and iron hooks for feet and lives in trees.

"The African man was a slave on the Saint Joseph estate, he was Ejisu Juaben she said, they called him

Juaben, he died some years ago, very old. Dabéline got all this from Miss Gauzhelm, the woman who was with the slave, she is still alive, she must well be over a hundred. Dabéline now has become the vehicle for these daemons, she is their product and it will be through her that this particular hybrid will continue."

"And she said 'Sasabonsam'?" asked Amé. Rosa nodded.

"And the mingling up of the African with the Gauzhelm tradition of Baltic witches brought about the power of flight and fire to this mixed-up monstrosity?" said Sidoné.

"That is so," said Rosa, "yes, everything we have in these islands comes from the mixture of black and white, all is traceable to the time of the formation of Creole society, right through these islands, right to the first period of slavery. What is good as well as what is evil comes from that shared past, look at us, we ourselves, the three of us, come from all that."

"Dabéline is in danger of death one way or the other," said Amé, "the people will kill her if they think that it is she, I am sure that they suspect her, that it is she who is the soukounyan. Her sister knows, that is why she convinced the priest to send for us and convinced us to come."

"Yes, you saw it last night, eh Amé, they came to you in the dream and in the flesh. The old crone knows we are here on account of her. She will come again, we have to go to her, the old woman is frail but the soukounyan daemon that she controls through Dabéline is very powerful, by nightfall tonight, she says, she would be possessed by that daemon. She would shed her skin, hide it, become a fiery substance, fly and find blood and bring it back for Miss Gauzhelm, that is why she live so long."

"Where is Dabéline, is she still at the father's house on Radix point?" asked Sidoné.

"Yes, she's there, she say, and so is Geneviève Gauzhelm."

That afternoon, before the sun began to fade behind the low hills to the West of Radix Point, their small party made its way to the old estate house overlooking the leap from which one hundred and eighty years before the last of the warrior chieftains of the Arenas had hurled themselves after murdering the Spanish Missionaries of the Capuchin order who had attempted to convert them to an incomprehensible religion dedicated to crucified life.

André Joachim, Evan Popwell, Amadé Frontin and Sidoné were armed with Lee-Enfield bolt-action, magazine-fed, repeating rifles that contained in their magazines one bullet each, mounted with a silver cap obtained from the melting down of twenty-seven silver British Half Crowns.

The storm promised from the night before broke with lightning speed that cracked the battleship-black sky and walked on jagged stilt-like legs on the horizon's Eastern edges. The deserted house greeted them with the slams of windows caused by the wind, obstinate and un-welcoming, its hard grey wooden front door locked and barred.

Circling round the back, the men gained entrance by breaking through the kitchen wall. Walking ahead of the two women, rifles at the ready, they came upon a scene of dereliction.

La Sirène Rosa's and Amélie's shaky voices could just be heard reciting the one hundred and thirtieth psalm as they made their way through the gloom; "De profundis clamavi ad te, Domine; Out of the depths I cry to you, O Lord;

Lord, hear my voice!

Let your ears be attentive

To my voice in supplication:

If you, O Lord, mark iniquities,

Lord, who can stand?

But with you is forgiveness,

That you may be revered.

I trust in the Lord;

My soul trusts in his word.

My soul waits for . . . ."

Before them sat Geneviève Gauzhelm, the witch, pale, balding, with wizened hands, mildewed eyes, dressed in rags, emitting ancient odours, a rancid, rotting breath and a heat that stopped them in their tracks as though they had entered an open oven.

"Shoot!"

A blaze of fire flashed and filled the room, burning their faces, and blinding their eyes. Behind them appeared a hideous apparition of shredded skin and iron claws and teeth. "Shoot André, fire!" Bam, bam, bam,

Rosa saw the witch blown away as silver mounted rifle bullets tore into her decrepitude, she felt the claw rip into her cheek, slashing down into her breast bone. She saw Sidoné raise his rifle and fire into the bosom of a dripping, skinless form that vomited a vile odourous steaming stream. She saw Sidoné draw and wield a cutlass, severing the head that flew past her face, screaming her name, to fall before where she had fallen, face to face, the lips moved, Dabéline said:-

"Miss Rémy, you reach too late."

Evan Popwell and Amadé Frontin lay dead, the flesh ripped from their backs down to their bones. Amélie's dress, which had caught on fire, had burned her body and face as she ran screaming into the wind and the driving rain to fall and roll down the hill in the tall, wet para grass that surrounded the house. Getting up she saw the house, its interior ablaze, and Sidoné with Rosa staggering down the front steps, his trousers on fire, Rosa red with blood, André Joachim on his knees, his face in his hands, before the inferno.

◆　◆　◆

7. LA SIRÈNE ROSA

Tanti Rosa never fully recovered from the soukou-nyan daemon's appalling attack. This had struck both her physical and psychical centres. The wounds to her face and chest healed badly, causing her pain even after they were only ugly scars. The trauma marked her emotionally and, in a sense, spiritually too, I suppose.

I remember her as an old, brown-skinned woman called Miss Rosa by the servants and the people who came to see us. We called her Tanti at home. She occupied what was known as the little room in the front of our house on Belmont Circular Road, just off the front gallery to which it was connected by a door. The other door of the little room opened to my grandmother's bedroom. When I was little she would give me a six cent coin to show to the moon. And holding it up before the silver light, she'd sing in her old lady's voice: —

"Bèl lalin, mwen ka montwé ou ti pyès-mwen! — ba mwen lajan tout tan ou ka kléwé."

Which means: —

"Pretty moon, I show you my little money; now let me always have money so long as you shine!"

"Is that magic, Tanti Rosa?"

"Oui, naturellement, ma chérie."

I will never forget the Jumbie stories that she told on full moon nights, when the Town's electricity supply to the new street lights was turned off so as to facilitate promenading, courting, window-shopping, practical jokes and storytelling. Myself and my sisters Eugénie and Amélie would sit in the little room on Tanti Rosa's bed and she on one of the two old-fashioned carved chairs under the oil painting of her great-grandmother, the Countess de Molé, and she would tell us 'tim-tims' as they called them long ago.

"Is that really true, for-true?"

"Oui, naturellement, ma chérie. Every word."

As a young girl growing up I was fascinated by her, by her possessions, they were so original, her clothes, her jewels, her shoes, so antique. I rummaged constantly through her things.

"Is this really lion's mane?"

"Of course."

"Wow!"

"Don't say wow."

Tanti Rosa's massive dressing table contained all the accoutrements of her former trade. Curiously-shaped, cream-coloured ware vessels that may be filled with hot water and placed against pains or inserted into the sufferer's nether-parts. A device that was operated by the turning of a handle delivered an electric shock . . . .

"Leave that alone. Don't play with that."

There were various powders, multi-coloured and labelled for differentiation, 'man you must,' 'stay home,' 'the fire of love,' 'commanding powder,' powder for money, to quiet down people. Parcels containing a piece of a cow's hoof.

"What's this for?"

"Put that right back!"

Camphor balls, guinea pepper to drive people away.

"Don't play with that."

Packets of sulphur to dispel evil spirits, and others containing mysterious balls made of hair and bits of shells, both sea and egg, feathers, fowl claws and cra-paud bottoms pressed flat, still pushing out a choking odour after fifty years of embalmment.

"Don't touch your face!"

There were books on the magic arts, tied with hemp twine and tightened with leather bands, containing seals, stamped into red wax, so as to keep imprisoned the spirit forces held bottled up in them.

"Who you got these books from, Tanti Rosa?"

"That is not your affair."

You could find barks turning to powder, their pur-poses now forgotten, as their labels had disintegrated because of the fungus. There was a layer of fungus throughout the entire piece of furniture, inside the drawers, shelves, everywhere, except upon a wonder-fully crafted silver cup which she, Tanti Rosa, had used to administer her potions.

"Go and wash your hands, your grandmother is call-ing you."

I would rummage on a rainy day through this fasci-nating collection of old chaplets, scapulars brown and black, tracts containing novenas, recipes for protection or for offense, the sealing of people's mouths, for opening their mouths. I opened little silver reliquaries, my heart thumping, fearful of what might be released or rescued, or dispatched after a century to fulfil a mission. I would remain intrigued by her for years after she had passed away. I tried to read or half half-read the recipes for potions. Hallucinating prayers to Archangels written in an elegant hand in a little notebook, still in my possession.

I took care never to say any word—especially long, complicated ones—out loud, for fear of calling up anything. There were little cardboard boxes with silver medals dedicated to obscure saints to whom rushed devotions may be rendered in times of spiritual or occult emergency. Decorative crosses that could be tied to the legs of beds to fend off evil spirits. There were tiny cases made of antique silver that had strands of hair, baby's teeth, and the stubs of candles that had been burnt during the confinements of now forgotten mothers.

"Whose baby teeth are these?"

"Yours, your sisters, your uncle Sidoné's, your mother's."

"Why you have them?"

"Just in case."

"In case what?"

"Don't mind that."

Flasks that once contained Holy Water. Some reliquaries had lots of little semi and a few precious stones that had been prized from their gold settings so that the

gold could be sold to Mr. Edinburgh, the Jewish ped-
dler, when things had gotten tight.

From a previous century, there were beautiful lace
dresses, fantastic hats, amazing underwear, a vast assortment of empty perfume bottles, long white gloves turning a creamy yellow and the delicate porcelain hands,
wrapped in tissue paper, that belonged to a wonderfully
beautiful statue of the Blessed Virgin Mary that stood
about three feet tall and mesmerised with an indescrib-
ably sad expression. She stood on top of the oldest bi-
ble in the house, on top of Tanti's massive mahogany
armoire. The Virgins' hands had been removed so as to
save them from accidents, but would be remounted for
especial devotions. Her crown was still intact up until
the 1950s, this was made of fine gold filigree and decorated with a quantity of small rubies. The crown was
kept in a locked compartment in the armoire together
with seven heavy silver table spoons, patterned bow fid-
dle and thread with shell, hallmarked 'Dublin 1817'.

I found a gorgeous silver, heart-shaped jewellery box,
about seven inches long, and about two thick, decorated
with rococo patterns round its side, lined in red velvet,
with the initials of Josephine and Napoleon entwined.
There was a story that this box had been given to the
Count de Molé, Tanti Rosa's maternal grandfather, by
the Emperor upon his marriage to Marie Josèphe Rose
de Beauharnais, née Tascher de La Pagerie, in pleasant
remembrance of the days shared at the military college
that taught them both the secrets of gun powder and
artillery.

There was a daguerreotype of Tanti Rosa's mother and father. They sat so elegantly. Tanti Rosa's mother was a beauty. I was told by my grandmother that it was she who had charmed the old Count into parting with his heirlooms, and had passed these on to Tanti Rosa. I acquired them together with an elegant washstand upon which was a basin and ewer in silver, engraved with a crest.

There was as well a red amber or perhaps rose quartz stone, set in silver, with Tanti's father's monogram, L R. Louis Rémy, inscribed. There was red sealing wax, and sheets of letter paper with her name on them, and a lot of nibs. Objects for the application of cosmetics, and for the assuming of different personalities and genders.

"What's this to do?"

"Put that back."

There were a quantity of small blue bottles used to catch and contain evil spirits.

"This can catch spirits?"

"Of course not."

I do remember, though, seeing Mr. Marshall, who used to drive the trams for General Araujo, old, and naked as he was born, on his hands and knees, in his front yard, trying to coax invisible creatures, Jumbies, into a little blue bottle. What could I know, I was only a girl at that time.

◆ ◆ ◆

Tanti Rosa died. She sort of went out of her head, saw and heard cocks standing and crowing in the lattice work above the drawing-room partitions, and phantom forms coming and going. When she died it was raining. I was standing on the back steps together with François Morocoy who had belonged to her mother and had been born in George Street at the house next door to the Angostura Bitters factory, looking at the water pouring out of the broken spouting, when something silver passed before me or above me, whatever. I ran inside and told Grandma, Auntie Andrea, Miss Didier, Madame Voisin, Miss Ijuana, and Miss Bart, that Tanti Rosa had died. They all went into the little room. She was dead.

By the next day, she would be buried, but before that, the body would be taken over by them. Extreme Unction had already been applied – now was the time for the spirits. Pennies for her passage, scribbled notes, cryptic messages to other dead people, to previous popes, to Archangels, to empower the living, prayers addressed to the Blessed Virgin Mary as Our Lady of Sorrows, to whom she was especially devoted, to Saint Roch, Saint Jude, Saint Fatimatusia. Saint Prudentius Galindo (I was born on Saint Fatimatusia's day). The hearse came, four horses draped in black net, with black ostrich plumes. I heard the announcement for her death on Radio Trinidad, a marvelous addition to our household that was never turned off. Death announcements came over the radio every half an hour—such was the pace of burials in the tropics.

"We have been asked to announce the death of La Sirène Rosa Rémy. She was the daughter of the late Ursule Bridgette de Molé and Louis Rémy, granddaughter of the Count de Molé, friend of Amélie and Sidoné Nathaniel and of the late Claude-Ambrose du Vivier de Noailles of Paris France. The funeral of the late La Sirène Rosa Rémy will take place today, Wednesday, from the house of mourning, Belmont Circular Road opposite to the Carmelite Convent, Belmont, to the Cathedral of the Immaculate Conception, and from thence to the Lapéyrouse cemetery. Friends and relatives are kindly asked to accept this intimation."

At home they had passed me over the coffin from Kit Henderson to his brother-in-law Isaac Escallier and back. This was to prevent Tanti Rosa from coming back to look for me. She was dressed in mauve. She was buried at Lapéyrouse cemetery between her mother and her grandfather. I, who never missed anything, saw my grandmother place a fantastic object, a beautifully painted jar, into Tanti Rosa's coffin, that she had asked to be opened at the graveside, to the surprise of all, and solemnly make the sign of the cross five times.

"What was that?" I whispered to Grandma.

"Nothing that concerns you."

The silver cross that had been on her coffin was removed and brought back and placed on her small iron bed that she had died upon in the little front room. After the funeral, I slept in Grandma's room in her bed, a vast contraption of brass balls, finials, loops, hoops and stays, with an enamel in full colour depicting the Blessed Heart of Mary as part of the footboard decorations. She liked to keep the teester, a sort of roof made of muslin, loose-hung from the four white enamel and brass bedposts, and the mosquito net draped like curtains. The whole thing looked like a vast gypsy encampment.

That night I stared at the enameled rendition of the Blessed Heart of Mary, her sad Italian eyes, rosy lips, pale-pink cheeks, thick eyebrows, and pale hand pulling back her blouse to reveal her heart on fire, wrapped in a thorny crown of white roses. That night, the fowls in the guava tree outside of the kitchen window started to make a lot of noise. Grandma woke up to see a figure move into the room and to the side of the bed where I was sleeping next to her. In the half light coming in from the street light, she could see a form bending over me, reaching out to touch me.

"Leave her alone!" she shouted.

I awoke. The figure vanished. This happened several times. It frightened her and she tried her best to keep it from me. But because I had picked up a little Patois I heard something of the sort mentioned around the house. Years later, I asked her about it:

"Who was it, Tanti Rosa?"

"No, it was Zinga."

"Who is that?"

"None of your business."

Finis.

I am so glad to have written this story. It has lived with me all my life. You see, it is almost a true story. I have kept the name Rosa Rémy in the story in memory of Tanti Rosa, whom I knew as a child. I have tried to tell the story with my mother's voice, as she was close to Tanti Rosa, a little too close, my grandmother would have thought, I'm sure.

It was a very old-fashioned world, I think, that I grew up in; it was a household full of old things, old time ways and old women, who spoke French Patois amongst themselves, with their friends and with almost everybody else. Except me. I could not understand what they were talking about, and they never taught me or encouraged me to speak it. I think they felt that its time had passed, you know, and it was seen as a leftover from long ago, from before modernity overtook us after the Second World War, and that it stigmatised one as being real old-fashioned. Patois has been virtually disappearing since the end of the twentieth century, along with a great many folk beliefs and oral traditions as our nineteenth century, Afro-French Creole cultural memory became lost through emigration and immigration, as well as being increasingly eclipsed by other realities.

To tell this story I have had to rely on the works of Melville and Frances Herskovits, John Jacob Thomas, Lafcadio Hearn, Pierre-Gustave-Louis Borde, Patrick Chamoiseau, J.D. Elder, LeRoy Clarke, Wade Davis, Maya Deren, Pearl Eintou-Springer, E.L. Joseph, Hersketh Bell, Andrew Carr, Merle Hodge, Albertina Pavy, Fr. Anthony de Verteuil, Mrs. William Noy Wilkins and the Comte de Glenstrae, while all the time hearing the words of John Henderson, Peter Pitts, Clara Wharton, Hector Gellizeau, Angelique Romany, Augustina "Miss Fairy" Fournillier, Anita Tardieu and the Paramin storyteller Lumatte in my head. Not to mention the voices of Rosa Rémy, Améline Loshon, Margaret Besson, Ella Joachim and those of my father, Joseph Besson who was a great exaggerator.

Respect and homage to Henri Antoine (Papa Nani), André Bedeau, Corrie Nelson, Jeanvill Pierre, Ebenezer Elliott (Pa Neezer) and to other Hüto, 'fathers of the drum' who have kept the Orisha faith vibrant. Many thanks to Dr. Jo-Anne Ferreira for her invaluable and timely help with the Patois turns of phrase that enlighten and make enjoyable this story, and to Kelsea Mahabir for the proofreading of the final book. And importantly, to Alfred Codallo, who brought our folklore to life with his drawings and paintings. In anticipation of their generosity I would like to express my gratitude to all the above. I hope I have not helped myself too lavishly from their words and their works, but I needed all the help that I could find so as to visit the imagination of those who lived in nineteenth century and tell a story of when our Afro-French Creole culture was thriving.

My wife Alice, generous as ever, has helped with the telling of this tale in all sorts of ways. Importantly, she listened with fresh enthusiasm to the indeterminable versions and the retelling of the many stories that she has heard before, and encouraged me to write this folklore novella because she felt that there was a need to keep our folk traditions alive, and this was a passably good method to achieve this.

Gérard A. Besson
'Tall Stories', Cascade
April 21st, 2011.